Stories, sayings, and scriptures to Encourage and Inspire

"拥抱·爱"系列双语典藏读物

hugs
TM

Korie & Willie Robertson
LeAnn Weiss 著

刘庆荣 译

for
pet
lovers

宠物总动员

U0105658

安徽科学技术出版社
HOWARD BOOKS

[皖] 版贸登记号：1208543

图书在版编目（ＣＩＰ）数据

拥抱·爱.宠物总动员：英汉对照/（美）罗伯特森（Robertson, W.）等著；刘庆荣译.—合肥：安徽科学技术出版社，2009.1

　　ISBN 978-7-5337-4260-7

Ⅰ.拥… Ⅱ.①罗…②刘… Ⅲ.①英语-汉语-对照读物②故事-作品集-美国-现代 Ⅳ.H319.4：Ⅰ

中国版本图书馆 CIP 数据核字（2008）第 198269 号

"Simplified Chinese Translation copyright© [year of first publication by Publisher] by Anhui Science and Technology Publishing House
Hugs for Pet Lovers
Original English Language edition Copyright© 2003 by Korie Robertson, and Willie Robertson
All Rights Reserved.
Published by arrangement with the original publisher, Howard Books, a Division of Simon & Schuster, Inc."

拥抱·爱.宠物总动员：英汉对照

（美）罗伯特森（Robertson, W.）等著　刘庆荣　译

出 版 人：黄和平
责任编辑：李瑞生
封面设计：朱 婧
出版发行：安徽科学技术出版社（合肥市政务文化新区圣泉路 1118 号
　　　　　出版传媒广场，邮编：230071）
电　　话：(0551)3533330
网　　址：www.ahstp.net
E - mail：yougoubu@sina.com
经　　销：新华书店
排　　版：安徽事达科技贸易有限公司
印　　刷：安徽新华印刷股份有限公司
开　　本：787×1240　1/32
印　　张：6.25
字　　数：80 千
版　　次：2009 年 1 月第 1 版　2009 年 1 月第 1 次印刷
印　　数：6 000
定　　价：16.00 元

（本书如有印装质量问题，影响阅读，请向本社市场营销部调换）

给爱一个归宿
——出版者的话

身体语言是人与人之间最重要的沟通方式，而身体失语已让我们失去了很多明媚的"春天"，为什么不可以给爱一个形式？现在就转身，给你爱的人一个发自内心的拥抱，你会发现，生活如此美好！

肢体的拥抱是爱的诠释，心灵的拥抱则是情感的沟通，彰显人类的乐观坚强、果敢执著与大爱无疆。也许，您对家人、朋友满怀缱绻深情却羞于表达，那就送他一本《拥抱·爱》吧。一本书，七个关于真爱的故事；一本书，一份荡涤尘埃的"心灵七日斋"。一个个叩人心扉的真实故事，一句句震撼心灵的随笔感悟，从普通人尘封许久的灵魂深处走出来，在洒满大爱阳光的温情宇宙中尽情抒写人性的光辉！

"拥抱·爱"（Hugs）系列双语典藏读物是"心灵鸡汤"的姊妹篇，安徽科学技术出版社与美国出版巨头西蒙舒斯特携手倾力打造，旨在把这套深得美国读者青睐的畅销书作为一道饕餮大餐，奉献给中国的读者朋友们。

每本书附赠CD光盘一张，纯正美语配乐朗诵，让您在天籁之音中欣赏精妙美文，学习地道发音。

世界上最遥远的距离，不是树枝无法相依，而是相互凝望的星星却没有交会的轨迹。

"拥抱·爱"系列双语典藏读物，助您倾吐真情、启迪心智、激扬人生！

一本好书一生财富，今天你拥抱了吗？

For **Sadie**, who patiently practices her mothering skills on her little brother and sister and her Beta fish

For **Bella**, who brightens
each day with her smile

For **John Luke**, who opened our
eyes to the love of animals and
our home to a multitude of pets

For **Will**,
whose fun and
playful spirit
fills our home
and hearts

Contents

chapter

1

Your Pet,
a Partner

1

你的宠物，你的伙伴

书及此笺，爱记住是我给予了你感动，与永远爱护你。

你记万都可以承受，因为我给予了你力量。没有什么可以……

……和爱的……之爱福窝！不管你有什么艰难险阻，有了……

……爱的……，终将成功。

亲助你的，

天女

——源自《诗篇》121:1-2；《绯立比书》4:13；

《罗马书》8:31,35-37

Look up and remember that your help comes from Me. I am for you! You can do all things because I strengthen you. Nothing can ever separate you from My amazing love! Whatever your difficulty or obstacle, with My help, you will triumph.

Helping you,
Your Heavenly Father

—from Psalm 121:1–2; Philippians 4:13; Romans 8:31, 35–37

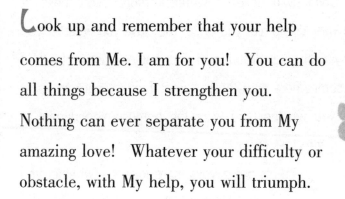

What makes a pet such a good friend? Could it be that pets don't care about the things that seem to matter so much to humans? They don't even notice how much money you make or what kind of car you drive. They love you whether you were the valedictorian of your senior class or finished somewhere near the bottom. They accept and value you whether you were the homecoming queen[1] or the class clown.

Pets are always there for you—whether you won the account that would make your company a huge sum of money or you forgot to make the call and lost the deal. Whether you're still happily married to your high school sweetheart or you've just been through a painful divorce.

Have you ever heard your dog spreading the latest gossip? Did your bird treat you differently after you lost your job? Has your cat made fun of you because you've put on a few extra pounds?

Of course not, and here's why: A pet's love comes without conditions. Above all else, pets are accepting and loyal. How wonderful to have someone or something that loves you and is there for you on your good days as well as your bad. Ever wish you had more friends like that? Have you ever wished you could be a friend like that? With your pet, you can enjoy one of the most rewarding relationships in life. You can have—and be—a partner.

是什么让宠物成为这么好的朋友？

是因为宠物对人类特别看重的事情毫不在乎吗？

他们甚至都不会在意你挣了多少钱或是开的什么车。不管你是毕业班代表毕业生致词的优异生还是勉强毕业的差等生，他们爱戴你。不管你是返校节女王*还是班上的耍宝人物，他们接受你，珍视你。

宠物永远为你守候——不管你赢得了一个能为公司带来巨大收益的客户，还是忘记了打电话而失去了这笔交易。不管你仍然和你的高中情人幸福地生活在一起，还是刚刚痛苦离异。

你曾经听说过你的爱犬四处散播流言蜚语吗？你的爱鸟在你丢了工作之后对你另眼相对了吗？你的爱猫会因为你长重了几磅而取笑你吗？

当然不会，原因就是：宠物的

爱没有任何条件。更重要的是，宠物对你敞开心

扉，忠贞不贰。不管在你得意之日还是沮丧之时，都有

某人或某物爱戴你、等候你，那是多么美妙的事啊！你曾

期待过有更多像那样的朋友吗？你曾希望你能成为那样的

朋友吗？有了宠物，你就可以拥有一段人生中最值得的经

历。你能拥有——也能成为——一个伙伴。

返校节女王 *(Homecoming queen)：返校节女王。返校节是

美国许多高中和大学在每年秋天所举行的庆祝活动。

为了庆祝老校友们回归以及新生的加入，大家

在一起举行盛大宴会，并在宴会中选举出

一个女生加冕为"返校节女王"。这个

女王乘着车游行，并以此拉开

体育比赛的序幕，通常

是美式橄榄球

比赛。

动物是极易相处的朋友——他们从来不提问，也不会批评。

——乔治·艾略特

Animals are such agreeable friends—
they ask no questions,
they pass no criticisms.

◆

GEORGE ELIOT

Snapshots

"Smile," Cheryl pleaded, trying to sound cheerful. She snapped a picture of her daughter. The beautiful little girl stood sad and alone in front of the flag—in stark contrast to the festively adorned school gym. Each year it was the same. The awards ceremony and celebration on the last day of school was never the fun, special day it should be—the way it was for other kids.

Most girls in the class were busy hugging each other, saying their good-byes, and making plans to play together throughout the summer. Some proudly held or showed off the achievement awards they had just won. But Mattie stood empty-handed—just as she had the year before...and the year before that. Standing quietly to the side, Mattie looked at the floor and fidgeted awkwardly with her empty hands.

Mattie never won any achievement awards. Those weren't given to the child who had barely passed third grade and was still having difficulty reading. The teachers had finally identified the learning disability that was making school so difficult for nine-year-old Mattie, but that hadn't improved the way other kids treated her or the way she felt about herself.

"I think you did great, honey," Cheryl encouraged her daughter, smoothing the little girl's hair in a protective, motherly gesture. Mattie smiled bravely, but she didn't look convinced.

"You know, your dad and I are very proud of you whether you got an award or not." Cheryl wished she could wave a magic wand to make it all better. She and her husband, Brandon, knew their daughter was smart, sweet, and kind. They just couldn't seem to find an arena in which she could succeed. Scholastics wasn't it, and they'd tried music, sports, and drama—all without success. It was evident that Mattie's self-esteem was suffering.

Mattie never asked permission for friends to come home after school and was never invited to other girls' houses. She spent much of her time alone, playing in her room, daydreaming, and drawing.

Cheryl and Brandon each took one of Mattie's hands and walked with her on last time to her classroom to thank the teacher and gather Mattie's supplies and papers to take home. Cheryl's eye was drawn to a beautiful painting of a horse displayed on the art wall. She was surprised and pleased to see that it was Mattie's work. Technically, it seemed superior to the other kids' pictures of houses, schools, people, and cars. But what most stood out to Cheryl was the feeling Mattie had captured. The chestnut horse ran alone. It looked wild, defiant, proud, and noble.

Cheryl had to suppress a gasp. In a moment she'd glimpsed Mattie's noble spirit in the image of the horse:

defiantly struggling against feelings of worthlessness; running as hard as she could, but unable to escape the prison of her disabilities; alone.

Cheryl resolved to find a way to release the wild, yearning spirit within her daughter to run free and proud.

◆

Cheryl didn't have to tell Mattie to smile as she snapped her daughter's picture atop the beautiful quarter horse. Mattie's ear-to-ear grin hadn't left her face since the moment she saw her dad leading her very special birthday present down the driveway.

"His name is Cinnamon," Brandon said proudly, "and he's yours." Mattie's mouth had dropped, eyes practically popping out of her head, and a squeal of sheer delight let Cheryl and Brandon know exactly how successful their gift had been. Mattie hugged both her parents tightly, then Brandon helped her climb into the saddle.

"We got him from the riding school down the road," Cheryl explained. "He has had some foot problems, so

16

he'll never be able to run as fast as other horses," she warned her infatuated daughter.

"I don't care," Mattie announced decisively, admiring Cinnamon's long mane and chestnut brown coat. "I think he's perfect." Mattie leaned down to address the horse. "Cinnamon, you're absolutely the most beautiful horse in the whole world."

"We also scheduled riding lessons for you and Cinnamon," Brandon chimed in. "Before long, you just may turn into a real horsewoman."

Mattie was hardly listening. She pressed her cheek against Cinnamon's strong neck with an expression of love. The large animal made soft sounds in return, gently responding to the young girl. "Hey, he likes me! " Mattie cried with surprised delight.

Cheryl and Brandon stood with arms around each other. Cheryl's eyes were filled with tears, and she could tell Brandon was battling a lump in his throat. Cheryl had a good feeling—and a whole lot of hope—that Cinnamon would be just what their daughter needed.

◆

Cheryl stood, camera in hand, waiting for the crowd to die down so she could snap another picture of the barrel-racing champion atop her amazing horse. Mattie looked beautiful in the red, white, and blue sequined costume Cheryl had made for her daughter's special day.

The rodeo had just ended with Mattie and Cinnamon circling the arena, carrying the American flag. This was an honor bestowed only on the best riders, and in the past few years, Mattie had become just that.

Mattie's entire class had turned out to see their friend compete in the state barrel-racing competition. "We're all here! " she heard Mattie's teacher announce proudly. Cheryl knew the teacher had spread the word and organized the seventh graders to come watch their friend at this special competition. Mattie's classmates pushed exuberantly to the front of the arena to congratulate the young star on her latest victory.

"Wow, you were great! " Cheryl heard a girl in Mattie's class exclaim with enthusiasm. "Will you teach me how to ride?"

"Could I have your autograph?" a boy asked shyly.

Cheryl and Brandon couldn't have been more thrilled for their daughter. The shy, self-conscious girl from just three years before was long gone. Cheryl knew that much of the credit for Mattie's turnaround belonged to Cinnamon—the beautiful horse Mattie sat on, patting proudly.

A low whistle of appreciation broke Cheryl's reverie and made her aware of a man standing at her left elbow. It was Mr. Cooper, the stable owner.

"They make a great team," Cheryl said. "They seem to bring out the best in one another." She kept her eyes on Mattie, who, in spite of all the commotion and adulation, lovingly, leaned down to gently kiss the animal and friend she adored.

"I can't believe that's the little chestnut with the foot problems," Cooper said, shaking his head. "I never thought he could be a champion."

"Mattie believed in him," Cheryl said, with tears of

joy moistening the corners of her eyes. "Sometimes that's all it takes."

"I guess so." Cooper nodded agreeably. "Still, a state champion ... If I'd have known he'd turn out this good, I never would have sold him to you—at least not so cheap." He smiled as he said it.

Brandon put his arm around his wife's waist, and they watched as reporters' cameras flashed brightly and Mattie smiled radiantly and posed obligingly atop Cinnamon. Looking confident, strong, and noble, she held the flag proudly at her side.

Cheryl dabbed away happy tears and raised her camera to her eye. This was a snapshot she didn't want to miss.

"笑一下，"谢里尔尽量用高兴的口吻恳求道。她给女儿照了一张相。美丽的小女孩一个人悲伤地站在旗帜前——和在节日装扮下的学校体育馆形成了鲜明的对比。每年都一样。学校最后一天的颁奖典礼和庆祝会一点都不像对其他孩子那样有趣和特殊。

班上大多数女孩都忙于互相拥抱、道别，计划着暑假一起游玩。还有一些女孩骄傲地握着或是炫耀着她们刚刚获得的奖项。但是马蒂却两手空空地站在那儿——就和她往年一样。她静静地站在一旁，低头看着地面，心神不宁地摆弄着两只空空的手。

马蒂从来没有获得过任何奖项。那些奖项不可能颁给一个勉强通过3年级并且仍然有着阅读障碍的小孩。老师们最终确定是学

第1章 你的宠物,你的伙伴

习障碍使得9岁的马蒂在学校很吃力,但这并没能改善其他小孩对她的态度或是她的自我感觉。

"我觉得你很棒,宝贝,"谢里尔一边爱抚着小女孩的头发,一边鼓励她。马蒂勇敢地笑了笑,但妈妈的话并没有让她信服。

"要知道,不管你有没有得奖,你爸爸和我都为你感到自豪。"谢里尔希望她有一副魔杖,可以让事情好转。她和她的丈夫布兰登知道他们的女儿聪明可爱、心地善良,但他们就是找不到一个能让她成功的舞台。做学问显然不是, 他们还尝试了音乐、体育和戏剧——但是都没有成效。马蒂的自尊心显然备受折磨。

马蒂从来没有提出过要让朋友放学后到家里来玩, 也没有其他的女孩邀请过她。大多数时间她都是自己一个人在房间里,浮想联翩,舞弄丹青。

谢里尔和布兰登一人牵着马蒂的一只手, 最后一次和她一起走进教室感谢老师,并将马蒂的日常用品和纸张整理好带回家。谢里尔的目光被展示在艺术墙上的一幅漂亮的马的油画所吸引了。她很惊讶也很高兴地发现,这竟然是马蒂的作品。从技术层面讲,它看起来比其他小孩画的房屋、学校、人物以及车辆的图画要更胜一筹。但更吸引谢里尔的是马蒂所捕捉到的那种感觉。栗色的马独自在奔跑,看起来是那么的狂放不羁、骄傲高贵。

谢里尔不禁倒吸一口冷气。刹那间,她从这匹马的形象中瞥见了马蒂那高贵的精神:独自一个人,奋力地和渺小的感觉相抗争;竭尽全力地奔跑,但却不能逃脱她那伤残的牢笼。

谢里尔决定要放飞女儿内心狂放、渴望的精灵,让她自由骄傲地奔跑。

◆

谢里尔给骑在漂亮的夸特马上的女儿拍照时,再也不用提醒她微笑。马蒂自从看到她爸爸将这份特别的生日礼物牵到马路上时,就已经高兴得合不拢嘴了。

"他的名字叫辛纳蒙," 布兰登自豪地说,"从现在起他就是你的了。"马蒂惊讶地张大了嘴巴,眼珠都差点掉出来了,喜悦的尖叫让谢里尔和布兰登确信,他们挑选的礼物是多么的成功。马蒂紧紧地拥抱父母,接着布兰登就扶她跨上马鞍。

"我们是在马路边的骑术学校买到的," 谢里尔解释道。"他的脚有点毛病,所以不能和其他的马跑得一样快," 她提醒了一下沉浸于喜悦中的女儿。

"我不在乎," 马蒂一边欣赏着辛纳蒙的长鬃和褐栗色的外

表，一边果断地回答。"我觉得他很完美。"马蒂俯下身对马说，

"辛纳蒙，你绝对是世界上最漂亮的马。"

　　"我们还给你和辛纳蒙安排了马术课，" 布兰登插了一句。

"不久，你就会成为真正的女骑师。"

　　可是马蒂几乎没有听见，她充满爱意地把脸颊贴在辛纳蒙健

壮的脖子上。这匹巨马也发出柔和的声音，温柔地回应着小女孩。

"嘿，它喜欢我！"马蒂惊喜地叫出了声。

　　谢里尔和布兰登拥抱在一起。谢里尔激动得热泪盈眶，她看得

出布兰登也尽力在克制自己的哽咽。谢里尔有一种很好的感

觉——也充满了无限希望——觉得辛纳蒙正是他们女儿所需要

的。

◆

　　谢里尔站在那儿，手里拿着相机，等待着人群退去，以便可以

给骑在这匹出色的马身上的马术绕桶冠军照一张相。马蒂身着谢

里尔专门给女儿的这一特殊日子准备的嵌有红白绿小亮片的骑马

装，看起来美极了。

　　马术比赛刚刚结束，马蒂手持美国国旗，骑着辛纳蒙在竞技场

上绕圈。这样的荣誉只授予最佳骑手。而在过去的几年里，马蒂正

是获此殊荣的人。

马蒂的所有同学都过来观看他们的朋友在全国马术绕桶比赛中竞技。"我们都在这儿!"谢里尔听到马蒂的老师自豪地喊道。她知道老师已经把这一消息告诉了大家,并组织了7年级学生来观看他们的朋友的这一特殊比赛。马蒂的同学用力挤到竞技场的最前面,祝贺这颗新星刚刚取得的胜利。

"哇,你太棒了!"谢里尔听到马蒂班上的一个女孩热烈地欢呼。"你能教我怎样骑马吗?"

"你能给我签个名吗?"一个小男孩羞涩地问。

谢里尔和布兰登从来没有像现在这样为他们的女儿感到兴奋过。3年前还羞羞答答、扭扭捏捏的那个女孩子早就不见了。谢里尔知道,让马蒂得以转变的大部分功劳属于辛纳蒙——马蒂所骑着的这匹漂亮的马,它正载着它的主人骄傲地慢跑着。

一声轻轻的赞许的口哨声打断了谢里尔的遐想,她这才意识到自己左肘旁站了一个人。他就是库珀先生,马厩的主人。

"他们是很好的一对,"谢里尔说,"看起来真的是相得益彰。"她一直注视着马蒂。马蒂不顾全场的喧嚣和骚动,充满爱意地俯下身,温柔地吻了一下她爱慕的动物和朋友。

第1章　你的宠物,你的伙伴

"我不敢相信,居然是这只腿脚有毛病的栗色小马," 库珀说道,摇了摇头。"我从没想过它会成为冠军。"

"马蒂相信他," 谢里尔说,喜悦的泪水模糊了眼角,"有时,这就足够了。"

"我想也是。" 库珀欣然地点了点头。"不过,全国冠军……如果我那时知道它会表现得这么好,我绝对不会把它卖给你——至少不会这么便宜。" 他笑着说。

布兰登一手搂住了妻子的腰。他们注视着记者的闪光灯耀眼地闪动,注视着马蒂灿烂地微笑,并在马背上亲切地摆好姿势。她手里骄傲地握着国旗,看起来是那么的自信、坚强和高贵。

谢里尔抹掉了幸福的泪水,举起了相机。这个精彩瞬间她可不想错过。

Your Pet,
a Teacher

2

你的宠物，你的良师

凡活物的生命和人类的气息都在我手中。你要通过观察我亲手所作的走兽、飞鸟、自然和鱼来学习。我要教导你，指示你当行的路。我要定睛在你身上劝诫你。

指引你的

造物主

——源自《约伯记》12:7-10；《诗篇》32:8

In My hand is the life of every creature and the breath of all people. Learn by observing My handiwork in the animals, the birds, nature, and the fish. I'll instruct you and teach you in the way you should go. I'll counsel you and watch over you.

Guiding you,
Your Creator

—from Job 12:7–10; Psalm 32:8

Have you ever seen yourself in your pet?

Perhaps you've noticed this strange phenomenon: After a period of being together, people and the pets they love often start to look alike.   You may even have discussed it around the dinner table with your family.   Maybe that bulldog didn't look like your uncle Fritz when he first joined the family, but after years together, everyone begins to wonder if he's not a long-lost brother.

Or perhaps we choose the animals that look like us physically or share common personality traits.   You may have known the talkative, older lady who bought herself a chattering bird, or the soft-spoken girl who adores her gentle bunny.

You've probably seen the active little boy who spends

every waking moment outside running and jumping with his energetic puppy. You might even be the strong-willed, independent girl with the stubborn cat.

Sometimes we learn about ourselves through our animals. Could it be that your pet is in your home to teach you something or to help you grow—to show you something about yourself you might never have seen otherwise? Who can say how we'll learn our next lessons in life—and who will be our teacher?

God teaches us things through all of His creation. Sometimes He uses the tiniest, gentlest, least likely of His creatures to fulfill His great purpose in our lives. Don't look past your pet; pay attention. You just might learn something.

你曾在宠物身上看到过你的影子吗?

也许你没有注意到这一奇怪现象:在交往一段时间之后，人们和他们所喜爱的宠物往往会看起来有点相似。你甚至可能在餐桌旁和你的家人讨论过这一现象。也许那只牛头犬刚到你家时，长得并不像你的叔叔弗里茨，但一起相处数年后,每个人都开始怀疑,他是否就是一个遗散多年的兄弟。

也许我们会选择在外表或是秉性上和我们相近的动物。你或许已经得知那个唠唠叨叨的老太太给自己买了一只唧唧喳喳的鸟，或是那个说话温柔的女孩非常喜爱她那温顺的兔宝宝。你也许还看到过那个活泼的小男孩只要出门，就带着他那只健壮的小

狗边跑边跳。你自己还可能是一个
固执己见、思想独立的女孩,养了一只性格倔强
的猫。

有时,我们可以通过我们的动物了解自己。你的宠物
有没有可能正在家里教授你什么或是帮助你成长——向
你展示你不大可能从其他方面获得的关于自己的东西?
谁能说出我们将如何吸取人生的下一个教训——谁
又会成为我们的老师?

上帝通过他的创造教给我们一些事情。
有时,他用他所创造的生物中最渺小、最温
顺、最不大可能被选中的,来完成他
赋予我们生命中的伟大的使
命。千万别忽视你的宠物,
要重视。你可能就
会学到什
么。

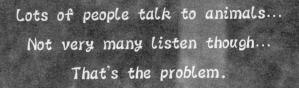

Lots of people talk to animals...
Not very many listen though...
That's the problem.

◆

PIGLET

(Benjamin Hoff, *The Tao of Pooh*)

很多人向动物倾诉……
却很少有人聆听……
这就是问题所在。

——小猪
（出自《小熊维尼的道》，本杰明·霍夫）

An Answered Prayer

"Leave me alone!" fourteen-year-old Alexis sputtered angrily. "I never want to speak to you again!" she shouted at her stricken mother. She slammed the bed-room door, narrowly avoiding hitting her cat, Whiskers, as she streaked into the room.

It only took a few minutes for Alexis's mother to appear outside the door, knocking quietly but with determination.

"Go away," Alexis warned grumpily as she plopped down on her bed.

"Alexis, don't do this to me." Her mother's voice was a mixture of pleading and warning. "I'm your mother. I love you...but you're hurting me."

Good, Alexis thought but was too smart or too kind to say. Part of her was glad that someone else was feeling as miserable as she was since her parents' divorce. Part of her felt self-satisfaction that she had the power to make someone else suffer after so prolonged a period when she'd felt helpless to stop her own suffering.

Another part of Alexis felt guilty—she knew the divorce wasn't really her mother's fault. She even suspected that she was taking out her own feelings of anger toward her father against her mother—the one within striking distance. But the suspicion didn't really matter. The anger and pain inside just had to come out. And her mom could be so...*annoying,* among other things.

"If you really loved me you wouldn't hassle me all the time...about my friends...about when I come home...about everything!" Alexis snarled through the door.

There was a pained silence from the other side. "I

do love you, Alexis," her mother said slowly. "When I express concern about your friends and your behavior, I am showing love."

"It doesn't feel like love," Alexis said with calculated firmness. "Is this how you loved Dad?" Alexis knew she'd scored a direct hit. Now silence on the other side of the door was total. Her mother was gone.

Feeling truly alone, Alexis pondered her last words. Her mother had told her many times that she loved her, but she had heard her parents say that to each other before. She rolled onto her back, taking in her eclectic mix of posters and a few pictures of friends and of her family—back when they were a family.

It made her sad to look at the picture of her with her mom and dad on their trip to the beach, taken just weeks before they had given her the news. Her dad had been so calm about it, like it was nothing—"Oh yeah, by the way, your mother and I won't be living together anymore"—like Alexis's whole life was not going to change forever with that one sentence.

Chapter 2: Your Pet, a Teacher

After the court hearing that gave her mom full custody, Alexis and her mom: had sat down and talked. Her mother had assured Alexis that even though she and her father were not together anymore,   nothing would ever change the way she felt about her only daughter. She had said that she loved Alexis—that no matter what she went through,   no matter what she would face in these difficult teenage years—her love for Alexis would never falter.

Her mom had spoken of the love God has for His children—unconditional love that knows no limits or end. "You can't separate yourself from that kind of love, Alexis,   and that's the kind of love I have for you," her mother had explained.

But the current situation made Alexis feel unsettled. She certainly hadn't been the easiest person to live with this past year. Could her mom's love hold up in spite of the horrible,   hurtful things she'd so often said to her? What had made her parents stop loving each other? Couldn't that same thing happen to their love for Alexis?

Alexis tried to wade through her tumultuous thoughts and feelings as she lay on her bed. Suddenly she felt the need for some physical reassurance, a loving touch or embrace...but she was all alone.

Except she wasn't really alone; Whiskers was there. Whiskers was always there. "Here kitty, kitty, kitty," Alexis cooed, trying to coax her feline friend to her bed to cuddle. Whiskers remained on the window sill.

Even she doesn't want anything to do with me, Alexis thought.

"Come on Whiskers...please?" she pleaded. Yes, the cat was always there, but sometimes she wouldn't even give Alexis the time of day. Whiskers just sat and looked at the teenager, with no intention of moving. Alexis, just as stubborn as her cat, was not about to go over and pick her up. Instead she made it a battle of wills.

"Whiskers, if you love me, you will come over here," Alexis said firmly. As if an ultimatum would bring the aloof cat running to her side. Whiskers just narrowed her eyes and stared at Alexis.

"OK, fine, I don't love you either," Alexis said sulkily. Tears stung her eyes. She knew even as she said it that it wasn't true. She knew she would love Whiskers even if the cat never came to her, never obeyed her commands... or even if she could have yelled hurtful things at Alexis and then didn't speak to her for days.

Suddenly it felt like a light went on in Alexis's head. Everything changed. Alexis saw herself in the white cat sitting on the window sill, ignoring the one who loved her most. She was hurt by Whiskers's action, but she loved her nonetheless. Was that the way her mother felt about her?

She was able to see clearly the kind of love her mother had told her about. Arguments, harsh words, fear, and resentment had drowned out these words over the past year, but now, lying there on her bed, Alexis suddenly heard them loud and clear. They spoke to her heart and set her free. She had been afraid her mother would stop loving her, but she never would. Alexis didn't have to test that love, prove it, or push it away for fear of being hurt when she lost it. Her mother would always love her—no matter what. How had she not seen it before? That's what her mother had been telling—no, showing her—all along.

The young girl cried for a while, wondering how to mend the fences, to tear down the walls she had been building brick by brick for so long. Then slowly she got up from her bed and walked to the cat that had taught her the lesson a thousand words hadn't fully taught. She picked up Whiskers. The cat purred and rubbed her face into Alexis's chest as though she understood the significance of the moment.

Alexis carried her cat through the house as she went to retake things right with her mother. She found her lying on the bed in her own room, gazing up at her ceiling in the same pose Alexis had been in just moments before. It was clear she had been crying.

Alexis handed Whiskers to her mother as one would hand over a peace offering, then lay down on the bed at her mother's side.   "I love you,"   she whispered as she grasped her mother's hand.

Her mother turned to look at Alexis,   a mixture of hope and shock in her red-rimmed eyes. "I love you too," her mother said with great feeling and gratitude.

Repeating those simple words over and over, Alexis's mother held her daughter tightly, tenderly kissing her cheek. Confused but overjoyed, she wondered what had brought about her daughter's sudden change of heart. Then, remembering what she had been doing just minutes before while lying on her bed alone,   she thanked God for answering her prayer.

应验的祈祷

"别管我！"14岁的亚历克西斯气急败坏地喊道。"我再也不想和你讲话了！"她对她生病的妈妈大声嚷嚷。她把房门砰的一下关上了，差点没把她那飞快跑进房的猫咪给夹住。

只过了几分钟，亚历克西斯的妈妈就到了门外，轻柔但坚定地敲着门。

"走开，"亚历克西斯警告道，扑通一下倒在床上。

"亚历克西斯，别这样对我。"她妈妈的声音里夹杂着请求和警告。"我是你的妈妈。我爱你……但你却在伤害我。"

太好了，亚历克西斯心想，但却太过聪明没有说或是不忍心说出来。她内心有一部分感到很高兴，因为自她父母离异后，还有其

他人也感到悲惨。内心有一部分感到洋洋自得，因为当她感到无助，无法停止内心所受的折磨，且过了这么长时间之后，她还有能力让别人感到痛苦。

亚历克西斯内心还有一部分感到内疚——她知道，离婚并不真正是她妈妈的错。她甚至开始怀疑，自己把对父亲的怨气发在妈妈身上——这个近在咫尺的人身上。但怀疑也不起作用，她内心的怒气和痛苦要宣泄出来。而她妈妈除了别的事情之外，有时又是那么的……令人讨厌。

"如果你真的爱我，就不会总是烦我……问我朋友的事……问我几点钟回家……问我所有的事！"亚历克西斯对着门大吼。

门的另一边有一阵痛苦的沉默。"我是真的爱你，亚历克西斯，"她妈妈慢慢地说。"我关心你的朋友和你的所作所为，那是爱你。"

"可那一点也不像爱，"亚历克西斯故意坚定地回答。"你就是这样爱爸爸的吗？"亚历克西斯知道，她击中了妈妈的要害。现在，门外是完全沉默了，她妈妈已经走开了。

一个人确实感觉到有点孤单的亚历克西斯，琢磨着她刚才最后所说的话。妈妈曾告诉过她很多次，她爱她，可她也听到过父母

应验的祈祷

亲以前也这样相互说过。她转过身,拿出她所搜集的一些海报以及朋友和家人的照片——当他们还是一家人时的照片。

看着她和爸妈到海滩照的照片,让她很难过。这些照片就是在他们告诉她离婚消息之前几周照的。她爸爸对离婚一事异常冷静,就好像什么也没发生一样。"哦,顺便说一下,你妈妈和我以后不会生活在一起了。"——就好像有了这句话,亚历克西斯的整个生活永远都不会改变一样。

在法庭上听到将由妈妈来全权监护之后,亚历克西斯和妈妈坐下来长谈了一次。妈妈向亚历克西斯保证即使她和父亲不再生活在一起,也没有什么会改变她对她唯一女儿的感觉。她说她爱亚历克西斯——不管她经历什么,不管在她艰难的青春期里遇到什么——她对亚历克西斯的爱都不会减弱。

她妈妈还提到了上帝对他的子民的爱——那没有局限和尽头的无条件的爱。"你不能将你和那种爱分开,亚历克西斯,那就是我对你的那种爱,"她妈妈解释道。

但现在的情形让亚历克西斯感到疑虑。在过去的这一年里,她显然不是最容易相处的人。在她经常说出这种可怕的、令人伤心的话之后,她妈妈的爱还会继续吗?是什么让她的父母不再相爱?同样的事情难道不会发生在亚历克西斯身上吗?

亚历克西斯躺在床上,尽力理清她那激动的思绪。突然间,她感觉到需要一些身体上的安慰, 一个爱意的抚摸或是拥抱……但她却是独自一个人。

但她并不真正是独自一个人;猫咪还在那。猫咪总在那儿。"嘿,咪咪,咪咪,"亚历克西斯轻声呼唤着,努力想把她的朋友哄到床上,抱在怀里。但猫咪却还是呆在窗台上不动。

"即便她不想理我,"亚历克西斯心想。

"过来,猫咪……好吗?"她请求道。是的,猫咪总在那儿,但有时她却连招呼也不打一个。猫咪只是蹲在那儿,看着这个十几岁的小姑娘,丝毫不打算动。亚历克西斯就像她的猫一样固执,也不准备走过去把她抱起来。相反,她把它视为意志上的较量。

"猫咪,如果你爱我,那你就过来。"亚历克西斯坚定地说,就好像这最后通牒会让这冷漠的猫跑到她身边一样。可猫咪只是眯着眼睛,瞪着亚历克西斯。

"那好吧,我也不喜欢你了。"亚历克西斯悒悒地说,泪水刺痛了她的眼睛。她知道,即便她这样说,也不是真心的。她知道,即便这只猫永远不主动到她这儿,不服从她的指令……或者即便她朝它大吼大叫，说些令人伤心的话，然后几天不搭理它，她也会爱它。突然，亚历克西斯的脑海里好像闪过一道亮光。一切都变了。她从这只坐在窗台上、冷落最爱它的人的白猫身上，看到了自己的影子。猫咪的举动伤害了她，但她仍然爱它。她妈妈对她的感觉也是这样的吗？

她能清楚地领会妈妈以前对她讲过的那种爱。无休止的争辩、刻薄的言语、害怕还有怨恨，在过去一年里将那些话淹没了，但现在躺在床上，亚历克西斯突然能清楚响亮地听见这些话。它们和她的心灵相沟通，让她解脱。她曾经害怕过妈妈不再爱她，但她不会。亚历克西斯不用试探那种爱，不用证明它，或是因为害怕失去时受伤将它推开。她妈妈将永远爱她——不管发生什么。她怎么以前没有看见？这就是她妈妈所告诉她的——不，应该是表现出来的——一直是。

小女孩哭了一会儿，在想如何"修补篱笆"，如何拆掉这么长时间一块一块垒起来的城墙。慢慢地，她从床上站起来，走到给她好好上了一课的猫咪旁边，这是千言万语都不可能完全教给她的。她抱起了猫咪。猫咕噜了一声，把脸往亚历克西斯的怀里蹭，就好像她理解了这一刻的重要性。

第 2 章　你的宠物，你的良师

亚历克西斯抱着猫径直走出房间，去和妈妈重归于好。她发现妈妈躺在她自己的房里，眼睛直直地瞪着天花板，就和自己以前一样的姿势。很明显，她哭过。

亚历克西斯把猫递给妈妈，就好像递过了一件和平的献礼，然后躺到妈妈的身边。"我爱你，"她握住了妈妈的手，轻声说道。

她妈妈转过身看着亚历克西斯，红肿的眼睛里夹杂着希望和惊愕。"我也爱你，"她妈妈说，充满了感情和感激。

亚历克西斯的妈妈反复重复着这些简单的话语，紧紧握住女儿的手，温柔地吻着女儿的脸颊。她既迷惑又高兴，在想是什么让女儿的心突然转变。接着，她记起了就在几分钟以前她躺在床上所做的事——她感谢上帝应验了她的祈祷。

3

Your Pet, a Protector

3

你的宠物，你的守护

我是你的避难所，你的力量。我是
你在患难中随时的帮助。我的名字是你
的坚固保护台。义人奔入，便得安稳。把
你的苦恼给我，我会扶持你。我不会让
你倒下。我会吩咐我的使者，在你所行
的一切道路上保护你。

保护你，加给你的
主，你的上帝

——源自《诗篇》46:1，《箴言》18:10，
《诗篇》55:22；91:11

I am your refuge and your strength. I'm
your ever-present help in times of trouble.
My name is your strong tower of protection.
The righteous run to Me and are
safe. Give Me all your worries, and I'll
sustain you. I won't let you fall. I'll command
My angels concerning you, to guard
you in all your ways.

Protecting hugs,
The Lord Your God

—from Psalm 46:1; Proverbs 18:10;
Psalms 55:22; 91:11

Is your pet your protector? Maybe he didn't pull you from a burning building, and you don't need her to be your "eyes" because you can see, but your pets can still protect you. In small ways every day, the little things they do can help you make it through the difficult times of life.

Maybe you've never thought of it this way, but when your pet is there for you each morning when you wake up, perhaps she's protecting you from the fear of being alone. When he demands that you take him for his daily walk, he may be rescuing you from the stresses of the day. When you feel her warmth at the foot of your bed, she is sheltering you from the coldness of life. When you laugh at his silly antics, he saves you from the sadness that might otherwise creep into your soul. When he reminds you that he's hungry, he keeps you from thinking only of yourself. When she sits on the window sill—waiting—until you return, she saves you from feeling unappreciated.

Life isn't easy. Sometimes we need someone or something to protect us from the dangers of the world around us—to rescue us when we're drowning in the little things, or even in the things that aren't so little. God knows that. He's there for you, watching out for you, knowing just when you need His protection. Who knows, He may be sending your pet into action just for you!

你的宠物是你的守护者吗?也许它没有从熊熊燃烧的大楼中将你救出,你也不需要它成为你的"眼睛",因为你自己看得见,但你的宠物仍然可以保护你。在日常生活中一些细小的方面,它们所作的一些小事会帮助你渡过生活中的难关。

也许你从来没有这样想过,但当你每天早晨醒来,你的宠物都在你身边守候时,也许它在保护你,让你不会因为孤单而感到害怕。当它要求你每天带它出去遛遛时,它也许是要将你从一天紧张的压力中解救出来。当你在床头感觉到它的温暖时,它在庇护你不受生活的冷淡。当你取笑它滑

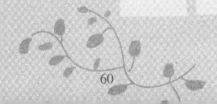

稽的动作时，它将你从不知不觉进入

你灵魂的忧虑中挽救出来。当它提醒你它饿了，他是

让你不要总是只想到自己。当它坐在窗台上——等

待——直到你返回时，它让你感觉到没有受到冷落。

　　生活不易。有时，我们需要某人或某事来保护我们

不受我们周围这个世界存在的危险——当我们沉

浸于一些小事，或者即便是一些不是那么渺小的

事情时，将我们解救出来。这些，上帝都知

道。因此他在那儿为你守候，为你保卫，

知道你什么时候需要他的保护。

有谁知道，他也许正是为了

你，而让你的宠物

行动起来

呢！

它是你的朋友，你的伙伴，你的守护，你的爱犬。

你是它的生命，它的爱戴，它的领导。

它将会是你的，忠贞不贰，直到它心跳的最后一刻。

——无名氏

He is your friend, your partner,
your defender, your dog.
You are his life, his love,
his leader. He will be yours,
faithful and true,
to the last beat of his heart.

◆

AUTHOR UNKNOWN

A Nudge
in the Right
Direction

Katy sat with her elbow on the kitchen table, forehead in the palm of her hand. She shook her head as she surveyed the mound of bills spread out before her, then looked out the kitchen window, hoping for some cheery sunshine to brighten her mood. Unfortunately, her view was blocked by a sink piled high with dirty dishes.

Since her husband, Phillip, died nine months ago, the responsibilities of running the household seemed more than Katy could handle. The older boys would be home from school soon, and she would have to figure out what to do for dinner. She just never seemed able to catch up anymore. The knot in her stomach tightened, and she choked back the tears that threatened to engulf her.

A slurpy tongue on her bare ankles jarred Katy from her discouraged preoccupation. "Oh, Gabe," she said with an emotional sigh, bending down to wrap her arms around the chocolate Labrador. "You have a way of knowing just when I need a little TLC." Tears were on the verge of spilling onto her cheeks when two of the boys arrived home from school. Even in the worst of times, Katy marveled at the gift of her children. Their deep dimples marked them unmistakably as their father's sons.

Jared strode into the kitchen with all the confidence of a firstborn. He flipped his sun-streaked hair out of his eyes and kissed her lightly on the cheek. "What can I do to help?"

I should be asking you that question, Katy thought, then smiled. She grabbed him for a big hug, amazed at how he always seemed to know when she was under too much stress.

Jonathan, her serious eight-year-old, plopped down on the chair beside her with a scowl that seemed to have become a permanent fixture. He was taking his father's death the hardest.

"How was school?" Katy asked hopefully.

"All right," Jonathan mumbled. Short, bleak answers were about all Katy was able to extract from her middle child these days.

Jonathan ran his fingers through Gabe's fur, and Katy noticed with relief that this simple contact was slowly lightening her son's mood. Gabe seemed to have the same effect on Jonathan as he did on her. Mother and son both found comfort in being able to touch the dog that had meant so much to their beloved husband and father.

Katy's mind drifted back to the early days with their dog. Phillip had been an avid sportsman and had purchased Gabe to train as a hunting dog. She smiled as she remembered her husband's funny tales of the active pup who would rather play with the hunters than chase the ducks. Phillip had quickly given up on training Gabe, and Gabe had become the family pet—a role the dog seemed to relish. He spent his days faithfully retrieving sticks, guarding the back door, and sleeping on the front porch of their country home.

Katy leaned over and took Gabe's furry face in her hands. She peered into his eyes, trying to send a message of gratitude for being the one constant in her life when everything else had been turned upside down. A lick on the hand was his reply, and Katy accepted it as a "you're welcome." Security was what she needed now, and Gabe, in his unassuming way, was up to the challenge.

Katy looked up to see her youngest son, Jake, toddle in from the playroom. "Jon-Jon! Jarey! " he yelled, grabbing each of his brothers at the knees. They gave him a pat on the head and headed for the refrigerator. Jake went with them, recognizing an opportunity for a snack. At two and a half, he wasn't quite big enough to get anything for himself, although he often tried. Katy and the older boys had gotten used to Jake's battle cry of "No, me! " whenever they tried to perform a task for him that he felt quite sure he could handle on his own.

Jake was a whirlwind of activity, but most days Katy was grateful to have her "little tornado" around the house. His smiles—and his messes—gave her mind a break from the frequent instant replays she still saw of Phillip's battered car.

Katy rose wearily from her chair and poured drinks for the boys. Today, performing even this smallest of motherly duties was difficult.

"Why don't you guys go outside for a while?" she suggested to Jared and Jonathan. "Jake would love for you to play with him, and Gabe could use the exercise."

"OK, Mom," Jared responded, always eager to please.

"Keep your eye on Jake," she reminded them as they closed the back door. "He can't swim yet."

Chapter 3: Your Pet, a Protector

"I'll try," Jared yelled over his shoulder.

The lake that had been appealing when she and Phillip had bought this house had proven to be a mixed blessing. It did offer some peace and tranquility: As she looked out her window each morning to a sunrise that cast beautiful shadows on smooth water, she often was reminded that God can calm any storm. Still, until Jake learned to swim, the lake would also be a constant source of worry.

Only minutes later, Jared and Jonathan returned with a tearful Jake. "Mom, he won't stay with us," Jared said, exasperated. "And me and Jonathan want to play computer games." But sensing her disappointment, he quickly recanted: "Never mind—we can watch him a little longer."

"No, it's fine, you guys go play." Katy knew the older boys needed time to themselves without a little brother always tagging along. "I'll see if Jake will sit down for a movie." She hated to use the television as a baby-sitter, but she had work to do, and it seemed no matter how hard she tried these days, she always found something to feel guilty about.

Katy settled Jake in front of the TV with his favorite video and resumed her unpleasant task at the kitchen table. Gabe rejoined her, flopping down on the tile at her feet. He was wet and panting from retrieving tennis balls the boys had thrown into the lake.

"Oh well, it was fun while it lasted, wasn't it, boy? Thanks for playing with them," she whispered affectionately.

A few moments later, Gabe got up and lumbered to the door. *He must be hungry or thirsty from all the playing,* Katy thought as she watched him go through the pet door Phillip had installed.

Halfway through the stack of bills, Katy felt a sudden uneasiness. The house was too quiet. She went to the playroom to check on Jake. He was gone!

Her heart sank just as it had the night she opened the door to greet the state trooper. She ran to the front entryway. Only a few days before, she had realized that

Jake had learned to turn the knob and open the door. She arrived to find her fears confirmed. The door was standing wide open.

Terrified, Katy raced outside. Her worst nightmare sped through her frantic mind as she sprinted to the back of the house, knowing Jake would head straight for the lake. Praying desperately that she would catch her little one in time, she turned the corner and came in view of the water. Her breath caught in her throat, and giant tears formed as she slowed, then stopped.

She didn't need to go any farther. There was Gabe, the family's loyal, loving dog, patiently nudging her youngest son toward the house. They were already halfway home. Katy shuddered to think how long this astonishing act of protection had gone on without her realizing it. Each time her headstrong toddler turned in the direction of the lake, Gabe blocked his path by putting his nose to Jake's side and gently guiding him in the direction of safety.

Katy waited at the top of the hill, allowing Gabe to

complete the job he had started. When they reached her, she hugged them both. Unaware of his recent danger, Jake wriggled to free himself from her grasp while Gabe, more receptive to her embrace, tried to dry off on her clean blouse.

Katy picked up Jake and, holding him tightly, walked back to the house with Gabe following proudly behind. Now as she entered the kitchen, the stack of bills seemed smaller. The pile of dishes didn't look nearly as high. Her heart felt lighter, free of the burdens that had troubled her just moments before.

That evening after dinner, Jared and Jonathan did their homework while Katy tucked Jake into bed and went to the sink to clean up. As she looked out the window, moonlight shimmered on some fading ripples on the lake. *Thank You, God,* she whispered as tears of relief flooded her eyes. She knew He had used Gabe to protect their family from another tragedy... and that He would indeed calm this storm.

千钧一发

凯蒂坐在厨房餐桌旁，手掌扶着额头，手肘撑在桌上。她一边审视着堆成小山一样的账单，一边摇了摇头，然后她向厨房窗户外看去，希望灿烂的阳光能让她的心情愉悦起来。不幸的是，她的视线被水槽里高高堆起的脏碗给挡住了。

自从她丈夫菲利普9个月前去世之后，打理家务的责任似乎非她所能应付。大儿子和二儿子马上就要放学回家了，她必须得琢磨出晚餐吃什么。看起来她再也来不及了。她感到胃更加难受，于是抑制住了快要将她吞噬的泪水。

这时，有东西舔了舔凯蒂赤裸的脚踝，让她吃了一惊，不再思索那些令人沮丧的事。"噢,盖布,"她深情地叹了口气,俯身搂住巧克力色的拉布拉多犬。"每当我需要一点温柔体贴的时候,你总是有办法知道。"正当泪水要溅到脸颊的时候,两个男孩放学回家了。即使是在最糟糕的时刻,凯蒂也会为她孩子的天赋感到惊叹。他们深深的酒窝让人一眼看去就是他们父亲的儿子。

贾里德迈进厨房,有着长子所应有的自信。他将眼前的一缕头发弹开,轻轻地吻了一下妈妈的脸颊。"有什么我能帮忙的?"

"应该是我问这个问题才对,"凯蒂想,然后笑了笑。她把他拽过来紧紧拥抱了一下,他似乎总是知道她何时感觉压力过大,她对此感到有点惊奇。

乔纳森,她那有点严肃的8岁的儿子,扑通一下坐在她旁边的椅子上,那皱着的眉头似乎成了他永远的特征。他对爸爸的过世最难以接受。

"在学校怎么样?"凯蒂充满希望地问。

"还好,"乔纳森咕哝道。这简短、苍白的回答,是凯蒂这些天来从她二儿子口中唯一能套出的话。

第 3 章 你的宠物,你的守护

当乔纳森的手指划过盖布的软毛时,凯蒂注意到,这一简单的接触慢慢缓解了儿子的情绪,这让她很宽慰。盖布对乔纳森好像有对她一样的效果。母子俩都能通过抚摸这条对他们亲爱的丈夫和父亲意义非比寻常的爱犬来寻求慰藉。

凯蒂的思绪又回到了从前和他们的爱犬在一起的时光。菲利普对运动非常热衷,于是买了盖布,准备把他训练成猎犬。她想起了她丈夫讲的关于这只活泼小狗的趣事,笑了。这只小狗宁愿和猎人们一起玩耍,也不愿去追捕鸭子。菲利普很快就放弃了训练盖布的念头,从那以后,盖布就成了家里的宠物——对这一角色,它似乎很喜欢。他整日忠实地取回他们扔出去的棍子, 为他们守卫后门,在他们乡村别墅的前门走廊上睡觉。

凯蒂俯下身,用手捧住了盖布毛乎乎的脸。她凝视着它的眼睛,尽力向它传递一种感激的信息,因为当其他所有的事都完全颠倒时,它是她生命中唯一持久不变的。盖布舔了舔她的手,算是回答,凯蒂将其理解为"不用客气。"安全感正是她现在所需要的,而盖布,用它那毫不做作的方式,很好地迎接了挑战。

千钧一发

凯蒂抬起头，看见她的小儿子杰克从玩具房里踉踉跄跄地走进来。"乔－乔！贾里！"他大声喊道，两手分别抓住两个哥哥的膝盖。他们轻轻拍了拍他的头，向冰箱走去。杰克也跟过去，知道有机会可以吃小点心。两岁半的他还不够大，不能什么东西都自己拿，虽然他经常在尝试。每当凯蒂和两个大孩子设法帮他完成他还不能自己处理的事情时，杰克就会大声呐喊，"不，我！"对此，他们已经习以为常了。

杰克是精力充沛的小旋风，但很多时候凯蒂也很感激有她的"小旋风"在身边。每当她看见菲利普那变了形的轿车时，她的脑海里总是会立刻回放当时的情形，而"小旋风"的微笑——还有他把家里弄得一团糟——都让她从当时的思绪中得以暂时的解脱。

凯蒂疲惫地从椅子上站起来，给孩子们倒饮料。今天，即使是履行母亲所应尽的职责中最微不足道的义务都是那么的艰难。

"你们为什么不到外面去玩一会儿？"她对贾里德和乔纳森建议。"要是你们能带杰克出去玩，他会很高兴的，盖布也能运动一下。"

第 3 章　你的宠物，你的守护

"好的，妈妈，"贾里德回答，总是想取悦妈妈。

"盯着杰克，"当他们把后门关上时，她提醒他们。"他还不会游泳呢。"

"我会的，"贾里德扭过头大声喊道。

凯蒂和菲利普当初买下这房子时，这个湖看起来很吸引人，可现在是喜忧参半。它确实能带给人一些平静和安宁：当她每天早上看着窗外的日出将美丽的光芒洒在平静的湖面上时，她总是会想起，上帝能平息任何风暴。但在杰克学会游泳之前，这个湖也总是烦恼的来源。

才过了几分钟，贾里德和乔纳森就带着泪眼汪汪的杰克回来了。"妈妈，他不愿和我们待在一起，"贾里德恼怒地说。"我和乔纳森想打电脑游戏。"但他似乎感觉到了妈妈的失望，又马上放弃了这一想法，"没关系——我们可以再看着他一会儿。"

"不不，不要紧，你们两个小伙子去玩吧。"凯蒂知道，这两个大孩子需要有属于自己的时间，没有小弟弟总是跟在后面。"我来看看杰克愿不愿意坐下来看看电视。"她很不喜欢用电视来当保姆,但她还有很多事要做,似乎这些天她不管怎么努力,总是觉得有一种内疚感。

凯蒂把杰克安顿在电视机前,让他看最喜欢看的录像,自己又到厨房去干那些让人不快的活儿。盖布又跟着她到了厨房,在她脚边的瓷砖上蹲了下来。他刚把孩子们扔到湖里的网球捡回来,浑身湿淋淋的,喘着气。

"噢,玩的还是蛮有趣的,是吗,小伙子? 谢谢你和他们一起玩,"她深情地小声说道。

过了不久,盖布站了起来,缓慢地走到门边。"玩了这么长时间,他一定是饿了或是渴了,"看它经过菲利普安装的宠物门时,凯蒂心想。

凯蒂整理完了差不多有一半账单,突然感到一阵不安。房子里太安静了。她走进玩具房看杰克,可他不在!

她的心突然往下一沉,就好像那天晚上开门迎接州警察官一样。她跑到前门通道。才几天前,她就发现杰克已经学会了扭动门把手开门。她到了门口,发现她的担心得到了证实:门大敞开着。

第3章 你的宠物，你的守护

凯蒂飞奔出去，惊恐万分。当她冲到后门时，那最可怕的噩梦飞驰般闪过她狂乱的脑海，她知道杰克会径直向湖边走去。她内心急切地祈祷，希望她能即时截到她的小儿子。她转了个弯，看见了湖水。当她减慢速度停下来后，她的呼吸霎时停住了，大颗的泪水涌了上来。

她不需要再往前走了。盖布，家里忠诚的爱犬，正耐心地将她的小儿子往家里顶。他们离家只有一半路了。想到这一令人惊讶的保护持续了这么久她都没有发觉，她感到不寒而栗。每当她那任性的蹒跚学步的小儿子朝湖的方向走去，盖布就挡住他的路，并用鼻子顶杰克，温和地指引他安全的路。

凯蒂在山顶等候着，让盖布完成他已经开始的使命。当他们到达时，她拥抱了他们俩。杰克还没有意识到他刚才的危险处境，挣脱了妈妈的怀抱，而盖布，则更愿意接受她的拥抱，想在她干净的罩衫上把身体擦干。

凯蒂抱起了杰克，紧紧地抱在怀里，走进屋里，而盖布则骄傲地紧随其后。现在，当她走进厨房时，这一堆账单看起来好像变小了。那一堆碗看起来也没有以前那么高了。她的心感觉变轻了,从刚才让她烦恼的负担中解脱出来。

那天晚上,用过晚饭,贾里德和乔纳森在做作业,凯蒂把杰克安置在被窝里,然后又到水槽边开始清洗。她向窗外看去,月光正洒在湖上渐渐逝去的涟漪上。"神,谢谢你,"她轻声地说,如释重负的宽慰的泪水像洪水般涌了上来。她知道,神正是让盖布保护了他们家免遭另一个悲剧……神确实会平息这场风暴。

Your Pet, a Comforter

4

你的宠物，你的慰藉

不管你经历生命中的什么苦难，即使是在生死之间，地震山摇，你都不必害怕。我和你在一起，用宽慰的洪水淹没你所有的苦难，使你可以助益他人。母亲怎样安慰她的孩子，我就怎样安慰你们。

爱你的，
慰藉一切的主

——源自《诗篇》23:4;《哥林多后书》1:3-7;
《以赛亚书》66:13

No matter what you're experiencing in life, even in the middle of life-and-death, earth-shattering situations, you don't have to fear. I'm with you, flooding you with comfort in all of your troubles so you can reach out to others. As a mother comforts her child, I will lovingly comfort you.

Loving you,
Your God of All Comfort

—from Psalm 23:4; 2 Corinthians 1:3–7;
Isaiah 66:13

Have you ever noticed that pets seem especially treasured by the really young and the really old?

As we grow older, pets often become our company and our comfort. Perhaps you've had a taste of this if you've ever felt alone or sad, and your favorite feline rubs against your legs or crawls onto your lap and purrs, listening attentively as you talk, offering his own special brand of therapy.

Kids love pets in a different way. They don't think about the time it takes to house-train, to feed, or to clean out the litter box. They just know their feathered or furry friends are there when they're hurting. A child will throw his arms around the broad, soft neck of a dog and let his tears fall into the woe-absorbing fur.

Somewhere between childhood and retirement, many of us get too busy to enjoy the benefits a pet can bring. But at any age, there are extra blessings to be found when we slow down a little and love a pet. We rediscover the comfort in a pet's company. So why wait? Embrace it now. Talk to your pets all you want, even if you look a little silly. Look into their eyes, cry, and hug them when you're feeling blue. Feel your stress ebb away with each stroke of their fur. And cherish them. You'll feel better before you know it.

你曾注意过宠物总是备受小孩和老人的青睐吗？

随着我们年龄的增长，宠物往往会成为我们的陪伴和我们的慰藉。也许你没有这样的体会，当你感觉孤单或是难过时，你的爱猫会蹭你的腿，或是爬到你的膝盖上呜呜叫，倾听你的谈话，向你提供他最特别的治疗良方。

小孩喜欢宠物有所不同。他们不必考虑要训练它们养成卫生习惯、喂养它们或是清理垃圾所要花费的时间。他们只知道当他们受伤时，他们的鸟类或是动物朋友就在那儿等着他们。小孩会抱住一只狗宽大柔软的脖子，任凭他的泪水滴在那可以吸入悲伤的软毛上。

在孩童和退休之间，我们中有很多人太忙了，不能享受一只宠物所能带给我们的好处。但在任何年龄段，只要我们放慢一下脚步，去爱一只宠物，我们就可以发现额外的恩赐。我们能在宠物的陪伴中重拾慰藉。那么还等什么呢？现在就开始拥抱。将你想要讲的话讲给你的宠物听，即便这样看起来有点傻。在你感觉悲伤时，凝视它们的眼睛，向它们哭泣，拥抱它们。你会感觉，你每抚摸一次它们的皮毛，你的压力就消退一点。珍视它们，你会不知不觉感觉好一些。

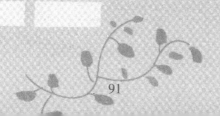

我对人与动物之间相互依附的力量从来没有怀疑过——能慰藉，能治愈，能激发，特别是能丰富生活。

——杰克·汉纳

I have never doubted the power
of the human-animal bond—
to comfort, to heal, to motivate,
and, especially, to enrich lives.

◆

JACK HANNA

Missing Mel

Merritt awoke with an unsettled feeling of dread. Where was she? What was this place? It was nighttime, and she was in bed, but even without her glasses she could tell the shadows were wrong—ominous. This wasn't home.

Was she visiting her son Kenny's family? No. Too many noises…lights in the hallway…unfamiliar voices in the next room.

"Mel?" she called out hopefully, groping fruitlessly in the darkness, grasping nothing. "Mel?" she echoed softer, uncertainly. She drew her wrinkled hand back to cover her trembling mouth. She could barely suppress a sob as the awful truth came flooding into her consciousness.

Oh, no! This wasn't Kenny and Sarah's place. She wasn't just visiting. She couldn't just pack up her things and go home tomorrow. She no longer had a home. She was in...in...that place. That place you went when you weren't quite done with life—but it was done with you.

Merritt turned on her side, buried her face in the pillow, and cried. She felt abandoned—utterly and hopelessly alone. She thought of Mel, but instead of bringing her peace, thoughts of him made her heart ache and her stomach feel hollow. Never again would Mel's sweet voice bid her good night or wake her with a song in the morning. Never again would she feel—

"Mrs. Henning?" Merritt's thoughts were interrupted by a woman's soft, kind-sounding voice and a gentle knocking on her door. Caught off guard, uncertain and embarrassed, Merritt said nothing, but she instantly ceased her crying.

"Mrs. Henning," the voice said again as the door

opened and light streamed in from the hall. "Are you all right?"

Merritt lay perfectly still as though she were sleeping, but through one eye opened barely a crack, she could just make out the fuzzy, large, dark shape she recognized as Nurse Rose.

"Mrs. Henning," Rose continued in a concerned voice hardly above a whisper, "I know you're having a rough time adjusting to being here. Woodlawn's a great care center, but it's sure not home."

Merritt continued to listen silently but with rapt attention as Rose sat in the chair beside the bed and leaned close, like an old friend or family member.

"I heard you calling out for your husband," Rose said conspiratorially. "I hear you calling every night." She paused and reached for Merritt's hand, squeezing it gently but communicating great empathy.

"My husband?" Merritt finally spoke, confused. "You mean James?"

Now Rose sounded confused. "I thought your husband's name was Mel."

Merritt laughed with genuine humor. "My husband, James, was a wonderful man. We had a good life together, and I *do* miss him." She paused while she sought the right words to express delicately how she felt about James. "But he died almost six years ago."

"Then who's Mel?" Rose asked, perplexed.

"My beautiful, intelligent... bright blue parakeet! " Both Merritt and Rose exploded in laughter and shared delight.

Rose gave a low whistle. "That must be some bird," she said appreciatively as Merritt nodded and squeezed Rose's hand back in agreement. "What happened to him?" Rose asked, almost reverently.

"Nothing happened to him," Merritt said sadly. "It happened to me. I got old. I got sick. I broke my hip. I can't live alone, and I can't ruin my son and daughter-in-law's lives," she sighed. "So here I am... cast off and alone while my companion, Mel—my best friend in the world—is shoved in the laundry room all alone at my son Kenny's house." She reclaimed her hand from Rose's grasp to wipe the tears from her eyes.

"I'm so sorry." Nurse Rose sounded truly sad for Merritt. "I'm sure your son is taking good care of him," she added, trying to sound encouraging.

"Kenny's a good boy," Merritt agreed. "He's trying to do his best for me—and for Mel. He never complains. But he has two young kids, and he and his wife both work. They can't really understand my silly feelings for a bird—even if he does talk to me…and whistle at me like I'm an attractive young woman." She let out a bittersweet laugh of appreciation tinged with regret.

"Did you ask if you could bring him to live with you here?" Nurse Rose inquired helpfully.

"Oh yes," Merritt said bitterly. "But rules are rules. No pets allowed."

"But he's just a little bird," Rose protested.

"No exceptions," Merritt said. "They told me Mel would be happier with Kenny's family and that I wouldn't have to bother with giving him birdseed or cleaning the cage. But you know, I think I miss that most of all—being responsible for something, caring for someone besides myself, being needed and loved." She started to cry again. "Every night when I went to bed, Mel gave me something to look forward to in the morning." She sniffed and was surprised to hear Rose also sniffling. "I miss him, Rose," she whispered, trying to stifle her sobs. "I miss my Mel."

"Of course you do, honey," Rose said soothingly, patting Merritt's hand. "We may not be able to fight the system around here, but you're not alone, dear," she promised. "Rose will sit here with you until you go back to sleep." Grateful for Rose's caring gesture and gentle touch, Merritt settled back into the bed and tried to go to sleep.

◆

Merritt awoke from a deep and distant place. Once again the unsettling confusion enveloped her conscious-ness. The sun was up. It was morning. Where was she? The sad feeling again: This wasn't home. The nursing home? But what was that sweet, familiar sound?

She shook her head to clear the sleepy fog from her brain. It sounded like...it couldn't be...? "Mel?" She fumbled for her glasses and settled them hastily on her face. "Mel?" she echoed hopefully. She looked around the sterile room that still didn't feel like home after nearly a month.

"Mel! " She practically screeched with delight. It was! It was Mel! Her beloved blue parakeet was by the window in his familiar white iron cage. He stopped his joyful song just long enough to greet Merritt with the phrase he had learned to mimic: "Good morning, Mel."

"Mel, how...why...who...what are you doing here?" Merritt tried to figure out what could have brought this turn of events. She moved as quickly as she could to get out of bed and over to Mel's cage.

Suddenly Nurse Rose was at the door, a broad smile showing off her pearly white teeth and dancing dark eyes.

"Rose! " Merritt scolded her fondly. "You did this—

but how? The rules…"

"The rules say no *pets*," Rose announced proudly. "But they actually encourage certified pet therapists! " Rose was practically beaming. She raised her hand to her mouth and whispered, "I certified him myself."

"You won't get in trouble?" Merritt asked, concerned.

"Nah," Rose reassured her. "After our talk the other night, I discussed it with the director. She agreed that a little 'bird therapy' might benefit a lot of the residents around here—if it's OK with you."

"You mean he gets to stay with me … " Merritt asked, hardly daring to hope. "Always?"

Rose nodded and grinned. "Always."

Merritt threw her arms around Rose in a poignant, grateful embrace. "Thank you, Rose," she whispered through tears. "Thank you for giving me back my comfort and hope. Thank you for giving me back my Mel."

想念梅尔

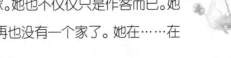

梅里特带着不安的恐惧醒来。她这是在哪儿？这是什么地方？现在是晚上，她躺在床上，但即便不戴眼镜，她也能分辨出这地方不对——不祥。这不是家。

她是在儿子肯尼家作客吗？不。太多噪音了……还有走廊上的灯光……隔壁房间里不熟悉的声音。

"梅尔？"她充满希望地喊道，在黑暗中徒劳地摸索着，什么也没有抓到。"梅尔！"她更加柔和、不确定地呼唤了一声。她缩回了起皱的手，捂住了颤抖的嘴唇。当这可怕的真相像洪水般涌入她的意识时，她抑制不住自己，抽泣起来。

噢，不！这不是肯尼和萨拉的家。她也不仅仅只是作客而已。她不可能收拾行李第2天就回家。她再也没有一个家了。她在……在那个地方。那个地方是在你的生命还没有完全了却而去的地方——但对你而言已经了却。

梅里特侧身躺着,把脸埋在枕头里,哭了起来。她感觉到被抛弃了——彻彻底底,孤独一人,毫无希望。她想起了梅尔,但想到它不仅没有给她带来平静,反而让她感到心痛和空虚。她再也听不到梅尔用它那甜美的嗓音向她道晚安或是在清晨用歌声叫她起床了。她再也感觉不到——

"亨宁太太?"一个女人柔和、亲切的声音和一声轻柔的敲门声打断了梅里特的思绪。梅里特感觉到有点措手不及,深感不安和局促,她什么话也没说,但马上停止了哭泣。

"亨宁太太,"这个声音又响起了,这时门开了,走廊上的灯光也照了进来。"你还好吗?"

梅里特躺在床上一丝不动,就好像已经睡着了一样,但从眯缝的眼睛中,她可以认出,这个模糊、高大、黑暗的身影正是护士罗斯。

"亨宁太太,"罗斯继续关切地小声说,"我知道你现在还很难适应这儿。伍德朗是个很好的养老院,但肯定不是家。"

梅里特继续静静地听着,但却全神贯注。罗斯坐在床边的椅子上,靠近了梅里特,就像是一个老朋友或是亲人。

"我听见你喊你丈夫,"罗斯策略地说。"我听到你每晚都在叫。"她停了下来，伸出手握住了梅里特的手，温柔地握着，但却流露出她也深有同感。

"我丈夫？"梅里特终于开口说话了，满脸疑惑。"你是说詹姆斯？"

现在是罗斯听起来有点疑惑了。"我以为你丈夫的名字叫梅尔。"

梅里特幽默地笑了起来，"我的丈夫詹姆斯，是一个很棒的人。我们一起度过了美好的一生，我确实想他。"当她寻找贴切的言语来细腻地表达对詹姆斯的感情时，她停了停。"可他6年前就过世了。"

"那么，梅尔是谁？"罗斯问道，困惑不已。

"是我那美丽、聪明……伶俐的蓝色长尾鹦鹉！"梅里特和罗斯都大笑起来，分享着她们的喜悦。

罗斯轻轻地吹了吹口哨。"那一定是某种很特别的鸟，"她赏识地说，梅里特点了点头，赞同地握紧了罗斯的手。"它出了什么事？"罗斯几乎是虔诚地问。

"它没事，"梅里特忧伤地说。"是我有事。我老了，病了。我把髋关节摔坏了。我不能一个人生活，可我也不能破坏我儿子儿媳的生活，"她叹息道。"所以我到了这儿……孤身一人，而我的伴侣，梅尔——我在这世上最好的朋友—— 一个人被落在我儿子肯尼家的洗衣房。"她从罗斯手中把手抽了回来，将眼泪抹掉。

"对不起。"护士罗斯真心为梅里特感到难过。"我相信你儿子一定会好好照顾它的，"她补充了一句，听起来令人鼓舞。

"肯尼是个好孩子，"梅里特对此表示赞同。"他尽他所能，做到了最好，对我——也对梅尔。他从来都没有抱怨过。但他还有两个小孩，而他和他妻子都要上班。他们确实不能理解我对一只鸟的可笑的感情——虽然他也和我说话……还向我吹口哨，就好像我是一个漂亮的年轻姑娘一样。"她露出一丝夹杂着感激和遗憾的苦乐参半的笑容。

"你有没有问过能不能把它带来和你一起在这儿生活？"

"噢，当然有，"梅里特苦涩地说。"但规定就是规定：不允许养宠物。"

"但它不过是一只小鸟而已，"罗斯抗议道。

"没有例外，"梅里特说。"他们告诉我，梅尔和肯尼一家生活在一起会更幸福，我也不用操心给它喂鸟食或是清洗鸟笼。要知道，我想我最怀念的就是那——要对某事负责，照顾除了我之外的其他人，感觉到被需要和爱戴。"她又开始哭了起来。"我每晚上床睡觉时，梅尔都让我第2天一早有所期待。"她抽泣起来，并惊讶地听到罗斯也在抽泣。"我想它，罗斯，"她轻声地说，尽力抑制住自己的哭泣。"我想我的梅尔。"

想念梅尔

"你当然想它，亲爱的，"罗斯安慰地说，拍了拍梅里特的手。"我们也许不能和这儿的体制对抗，但你绝不是孤身一个人，亲爱的，"她向她保证。"罗斯会坐在这儿陪你，直到你睡着。"多亏了罗斯关心的举止和温柔的爱抚，梅里特又重新上了床，准备睡觉。

◆

梅里特从一个深远的地方醒来。又一次，不安的困惑席卷了她的意识。太阳升起了，已经到了早上。她在哪儿？又有一种悲伤的感觉。这不是家。是疗养院？但那甜美熟悉的声音又是什么？

她摇了摇头，想赶走头脑里的困意。这听起来像……难道这不是……？"梅尔？"她摸索着她的眼镜，急忙戴上。"梅尔？"她充满希望地又喊了一声。她看了看消过毒的房间，在过了将近1个月之后，她还是感觉这儿不是家。

"梅尔！"她简直是欣喜若狂地尖叫了起来。是的！这正是梅尔！她那可爱的蓝色长尾鹦鹉就在窗户边，在它那熟悉的白色铁笼里。它暂停了它欢快的歌唱，用它学会模仿的句子问候梅里特："早上好，梅尔。"

"梅尔，你是怎么……为何……是谁……你在这儿做什么？"梅里特想弄清这到底是怎么回事。她飞快地下了床，跑到梅尔的笼子旁。

突然，护士罗斯站到了门口，明朗的微笑露出了她的明眸皓齿。

"罗斯！"梅里特温柔地责备道。"你这样做——但你是怎么做到的？那些规定……"

"规定是说不许养宠物，"罗斯骄傲地宣布。"但他们确实鼓励有资格的宠物治疗师！"罗斯其实已经是笑逐颜开了。她把手放在嘴边，小声说，"我自己给它发的资格证书。"

"你不会有麻烦吧？"梅里特关切地问。

"不会，"罗斯宽慰她。"那晚我们谈话以后，我就和院长讨论了一下。她也认为一点点'宠物鸟疗法'也许会让这儿很多的住户受益——如果你没意见的话。"

"你是说，它会和我生活在一起……"梅里特问道，几乎不敢抱此幻想。"永远？"

罗斯点了点头，笑着说，"永远。"

梅里特深情地搂住了罗斯的脖子，充满了感激。"谢谢你，罗斯，"她哭着说，"谢谢你，给我带回了我的慰藉和希望。谢谢你，给我带回了我的梅尔。"

chapter

5

Your Pet,
a Believer

5

你的宠物，你的信徒

你要专心仰赖我。要知道,当你追随我时,我会给你指路。我在所有对你的承诺中爱你,且忠诚守信。当你倚靠我时,我永恒的爱就会从四面环绕你。

忠诚的,
值得信赖的上帝

——源自《箴言》3:5-6;《诗篇》145:13;32:10

You can trust in Me with all your heart. Know that I'll direct your steps when you follow Me. I'm loving toward you and faithful in all of My promises to you. My unfailing love surrounds you when you trust in Me!

Faithfully,

Your Trustworthy God

—from Proverbs 3:5–6; Psalms 145:13; 32:10

The trust between a pet and his or her human is inspiring, if sometimes amusing. Maybe your cat jumps onto your chest before the alarm goes off in the morning because she knows if she meows long enough, she'll get fed. Perhaps your parrot keeps talking even when you've gone into the next room, because he's sure you can still hear him and will return with a piece of cheese—or anything to quiet him while you're on the phone with an important client.

There's nothing like watching a dog's ears perk up at the sound of your voice, listening and cocking her head as though she understands every word you're saying and believes it's of the utmost importance.

But have you ever bandaged a cut or cleaned out a wound and been amazed at how cooperative and trusting your pet was, even when he couldn't understand what you were doing?

Pets believe that we love them and will do what's best for them. That we're paying attention when they meow or chatter or bark and will somehow understand and meet their needs.

Similarly, we can believe that God loves us and hears us when we talk to Him. First Peter 3:12 says, "The eyes of the Lord are on the righteous and his ears are attentive to their prayer." When you're hurting or in need, just cry out to God— and believe that He's listening.

宠物和它的主人之间的信

赖如果有时看来很有趣,同样也令人鼓舞。也许你的猫在早上闹铃还没响的时候就跳到你怀里,那是因为它知道,如果它喵喵叫一段时间,它就有早餐了。也许在你走到隔壁的房间之后,你的鹦鹉还继续讲话,因为它相信,即使你在和重要客户在电话里谈话时,你仍然能听见它,并给它带一块奶酪——或其他什么可以让它安静下来的东西。

没有什么比得上观看一只小狗在听到你的声音之后竖起耳朵、仔细聆听,昂着头的样子,就好像它明白你所说的每个字,并且相信它至关重要。

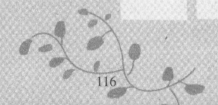

你曾包扎或清洗过伤口，并为你的宠物所表现出的合作和信任感到过惊奇吗？即便它不明白你到底在做什么。

宠物相信我们爱它们，并且愿意为它们做到最好。它们相信，当它们喵喵叫、嘎嘎叫或是汪汪叫时，我们在注意它们，并且以某种方式理解和满足它们的需要。

同样，我们可以相信上帝爱我们，当我们和他交谈时，他在倾听。《彼得前书》3：12写道，"主的眼看顾义人，主的耳听他们的祈祷。"当你受到伤害或是在危难中时，只管向上帝呼喊——要相信，他就在倾听。

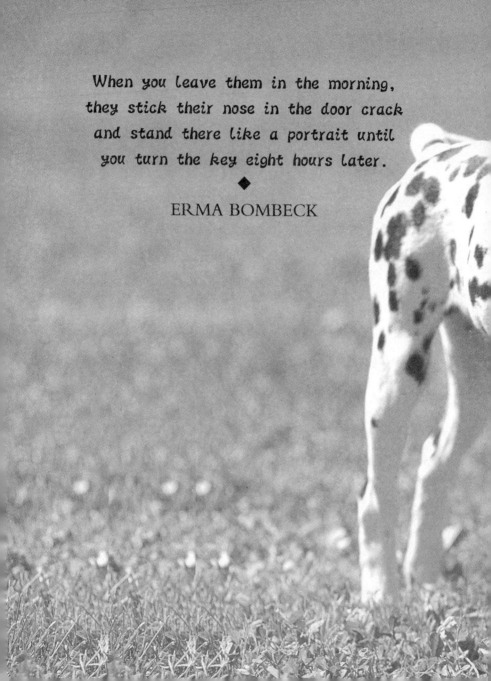

When you leave them in the morning,
they stick their nose in the door crack
and stand there like a portrait until
you turn the key eight hours later.

◆

ERMA BOMBECK

当你在早上出门离开它们的时候，他们会把鼻子塞在门缝里，像一幅肖像一样站在那儿，直到你八小时后打开钥匙。

——埃尔马·邦贝克

Little
Dog Lost

"We raised him right, Mary, I know we did," Kay said, trying to convince herself more than her friend as they drove home from a day of shopping. Alan was her younger son—the son who had always tested the limits and his parents' rules as he lived life on the edge.

"Of course you did," Mary replied supportively.

"I don't know what to do anymore," Kay confessed, discouraged. "Nothing makes sense. I can't fix anything. Everything I try to do or say just seems to push Alan further away."

"It's not up to you," Mary said. "You've done all you can. Now you just have to be patient—and believe it'll work out OK in the end."

That wasn't what Kay wanted to hear. "It's so hard to do nothing and wait," she protested.

"You can keep praying," Mary tried to assure her. "That's not 'doing nothing'. It's voicing your needs to the only One who has power to change things."

Kay sighed wearily. "It even feels like praying is useless." That felt like a dangerous admission, but Kay also felt relieved to have brought her feelings out into the open. She glanced at Mary to see if the revelation had shocked her, but Mary's face registered only compassion and support. "You know how many times I've been on my knees for him, begging God to change Alan's heart and bring him back home, but things just keep getting worse instead of better."

When Alan had finished high school, he decided he didn't need college or help from his parents—not if it came with any type of rules or restrictions. Now he was off on his own, living the "good life"—or so he seemed to think. Kay knew the road filled with parties, drugs, and alcohol was the road many kids take, but that was small consolation. She hoped and prayed Alan wouldn't have to hit rock bottom before he came to his senses.

"I've never felt this hopeless before," Kay confided. "It's a feeling of utter abandonment, and it's scary," she explained as Mary pulled into her driveway to drop her off.

Mary leaned over and hugged her discouraged friend as Kay opened the car door to get out. "Why doesn't anything change?" Kay whispered. A tear splashed on Mary's shoulder.

"It will," Mary said earnestly, squeezing Kay tighter for emphasis. "Don't you give up on Alan—or on God," she urged. "Keep believing. Keep talking. Keep the faith. Someday you'll see that you haven't been abandoned or forgotten."

Kay walked sullenly up the path to the front door with the same knot in her stomach and the same heavy heart she'd lived with for months now. Did she dare to hope Mary was right? Could she believe even when she felt so helpless and alone?

She walked inside to find her husband asleep in his recliner, a golf game playing loudly on TV. This was Phil's typical pose for a Saturday afternoon, but something wasn't quite right about this picture. She gently nudged her husband till he awoke, then kissed his forehead.

"How was your day?" Phil asked with a lazy smile.

"OK, I guess. We talked about Alan most of the time. It was good to have someone to talk to."

"Speaking of someone to talk to," Kay said, "Where's Jesse?"

Her family had always teased Kay about how she talked to Jesse, her brown and white miniature rat terrier. She regularly carried on a full, albeit one-sided, conversation with her beloved dog.

"I don't know," Phil replied, yawning. "He's got to be around here somewhere."

"He should have been out here by now." Kay had expected the little dog would have spent the afternoon with Phil—in his customary position on the back of the recliner, pink belly curled around the top of Phil's head. But no matter what, he *always* greeted her when she came home, jumping and barking as if he hadn't seen her in months even when she had only been gone for a couple of hours.

"Jesse," Kay called. She continued calling his name, checking all the little dog's favorite haunts before she started searching the house with a new sense of urgency. A mixture of dread and panic rose in her heart. *This isn't normal,* Kay thought. *Something bad must have happened.*

"Jesse! " Kay called worriedly. "When did you last see him?" she asked Phil, who had joined her search.

"I guess I haven't seen him all afternoon," Phil said, suddenly looking miserable. "But I can't imagine where he could have gone or what sort of trouble he could get into around here," he added hopefully.

They had only been looking for a couple of minutes when they first heard the bark. It was muffled, but they recognized it immediately as Jesse's.

"Where is that coming from?" Kay asked, concerned and puzzled. Then she heard Jesse bark again. It wasn't very loud, but it was definitely him. At least he was alive and somewhere nearby. Kay felt a little better. But where was he?

Was he stuck somewhere—in the fireplace, under a bed? Could something have fallen on him and injured him so that he couldn't get back to them? A jumble of half-formed questions and irrational fears tumbled through her mind as she ran frantically through the house, checking closets, bathrooms, nooks, and crannies—anywhere a little dog could possibly be. Again they heard the bark.

This time it clicked: "The intercom! " Kay and Phil cried in unison.

"He's in the shop! " Phil hollered. "I must have locked him in when I came in…over four hours ago! " Kay and Phil both ran out the back door toward the shop like lifeguards taking off for the big rescue.

Upon retiring, Phil had set up a woodworking shop

just behind their house. He had always loved working with his hands,   and although at first he'd intended only to make things for friends and family,   he now had a small business. The intercom system between the shop and the house made it easy for Kay to talk to Phil even when he was working. She would call him over for lunch or give him a phone message.

The intercoms also had proven a fun game for the grandkids. They talked back and forth as if on CB radios. Kay often laughed when she heard a "Ten-four, good buddy," or an "Over and out" from the speaker. But how was it that they were now hearing Jesse over the intercom? It didn't make sense, but that didn't stop Kay from racing to Jesse's side in response to his cries for help.

As Kay and Phil passed the shop's window,   they were astounded at what they saw: Jesse was standing up on Phil's chair. He rested one front paw on the desk, but with the other,   he was pressing the call button on the intercom while he tirelessly barked out his plea to be found. They had known Jesse was smart: He could shake hands or bark on command. But how had he figured out the intercom system? They were amazed at the ingenuity of their little dog. Even more, Kay marveled at the persistence and faith Jesse had demonstrated after being trapped alone for many hours. How long had he barked into thin air? Why did he keep barking when there was no response for so long?

When Kay and Phil burst through the door, Jesse jumped down and ran to greet them. He jumped into Kay's open arms and licked her face with gratitude and relief.

"Good dog," Kay repeated, hugging Jesse tightly and kissing the brown spot on his head.   "You know, Phil, Jesse knew we would rescue him." With tears in her eyes, she continued. "All he had to do was make sure we could hear his voice—he knew that would be enough for us to keep searching until we found him."

Phil nodded his agreement. Then, lightening the mood, he added, "You rescued him all right; I haven't seen you run like that since college." Kay slugged her husband playfully on the shoulder.

That night before bed, Kay prayed a prayer of thankfulness for having Jesse safe at home again. She scratched the little dog behind his ears, then she began praying for her son—the same prayer she had offered up a thousand times before. She had a new assurance that God was listening. The feeling of aloneness and abandonment that had weighed so heavily on her heart just hours before was gone. In its place was peace.

Jesse had never given up believing she would rescue him, even when it seemed no one heard him and no one came. New confidence and faith welled up in Kay's heart. Neither would she give up. She believed God heard her prayers and cared about her and about Alan. She would never stop praying and believing.

It would be enough.

迷失的小狗

"我们是尽力让他健全地成长,玛丽,我知道我们是。"凯说,更像是尽力在说服她自己,而不像是在说服她朋友。她们刚刚结束一天的购物,准备开车回家。艾伦是她的小儿子——这个儿子总是挑战极限和父母的规则,生活在边缘上。

"你当然是,"玛丽赞同地说。

"我都不知道还该做什么,"凯坦白道,非常沮丧。"没有什么有用。我什么事都不能解决。我每试着做什么或是说什么,都像是把艾伦推得更远。"

"这不是由你决定的,"玛丽说。"你已经尽力了。现在你只需耐心等待——相信最后一定会好起来的。"

这可不是凯想听到的。"什么事都不做,就这样等着,这太难了，"她提出异议。

"你可以继续祈祷，"玛丽尽力安慰她。"那不叫'什么也不做'。那是把你的需要交给唯一有能力改变事情的主。"

凯疲惫地叹了口气。"感觉好像祈祷也没有用。"这听起来像是很危险的坦白，但能把自己的感受找人倾诉一下，凯还是觉得宽慰一些。她瞥了一眼玛丽，看她的这一坦白是否让她震惊，可玛丽的脸上却只有同情和支持。"你要知道我曾多少次跪下来求他，求上帝能让艾伦回心转意，让他重新回家，但事情却越来越糟，一点也没好转。"

当艾伦高中毕业后，他决定不上大学，也不接受父母的帮助——这倒不是出于某种规定或限制。现在他一个人自由自在，过着"好日子"——或者他看起来是这样认为的。凯知道，这条充满了舞会、毒品和酒精的道路是很多孩子所选择的路，但这对她而言也是安慰甚微。她希望、也祈祷艾伦不会等到陷入谷底才醒悟过来。

"我从来没有这样无望过，"凯倾诉道。"这感觉就像是被彻底抛弃了，这很令人害怕，"玛丽停到路边把她放下车时，凯向她解释。

当凯打开车门准备出去时，玛丽俯下身拥抱了一下她气馁的朋友。"为什么没有任何事发生改变呢？"凯低声说道。一滴眼泪溅到了玛丽的肩上。

第5章 你的宠物，你的信徒

"会的，"玛丽真诚地说，为了强调她所说的话，她把凯抱得更紧了。"千万别对艾伦——或者上帝失去信心，"她劝道。"要继续相信，继续交谈，继续信任。总有一天，你会发现你没有被抛弃或是忘记。"

凯闷闷不乐地在路上走着，走到房屋前门，心中的结还是没有打开，仍然像几个月以来一样的沉重。她敢奢望玛丽是对的吗？即使当她感到孤独无助时，还敢相信吗？

她走进屋，发现她丈夫躺在躺椅上，电视里的高尔夫节目大声地放着。这是菲尔典型的周六下午的姿势，但眼前的这副图画似乎有些不对劲。她轻轻推了推丈夫，直到他醒来，然后吻了吻他的前额。

"今天过得怎么样？"菲尔带着倦意的微笑问她。

"我想还好。大多数时间我们在谈论艾伦。能找个人倾诉一下真的很好。"

"说到找人说话，"凯说，"杰西在哪儿？"

凯的家人总是取笑她和杰西——她那棕白色的小猎犬——说话的样子。她定期会和她的爱犬进行一次长谈，虽然是单向的。

"我不知道，"菲尔打着哈欠回答道。"它应该就在附近什么地方。"

"它这个时候应该在这儿才对。"凯原以为，小狗下午会和菲尔在一起——在它习惯待的地方，躺椅的后面，它那粉色的肚子绕

迷失的小狗

在菲尔的头上。但不管发生什么，它总会在凯回来时迎接她，跳着、叫着，就好像几个月没有看见她一样，虽然她出去才几个小时而已。

"杰西，"凯叫道。她继续喊着它的名字，到所有这只小狗最爱去的地方找，很快，她就开始焦急地满屋子找了。她心里夹杂着担心和恐惧。"这有点不正常，"凯心想，"一定发生了什么不好的事。"

"杰西！"凯焦急地喊道。"你最后一次看到它是什么时候？"她问和她一起寻找的菲尔。

"我想我整个下午都没看到他了，"菲尔说，突然看起来有点痛苦。"但我想象不出它会到哪儿去，或是在这附近遇到了什么麻烦，"他满怀希望地补充了一句。

他们才找了几分钟，就听到了狗的叫声。声音听起来有点模糊，但他们马上就听出是杰西的叫声。

"这声音是从哪儿传来的？"凯充满了焦虑和疑惑地问。很快，她又听见杰西叫了一声。声音不是很大，但肯定是它。至少，它还活着，并且就在附近的什么地方。凯感觉好一些。但它到底在哪儿？

它卡在什么地方了吗——壁炉里，还是床下？还是什么东西把它砸伤了，它不能回家？当她疯狂地在屋子里跑，检查壁橱、卫生间、角落——任何一只小狗可能待的地方时，一大堆模糊的问题和失去理智的担心在她脑海里翻滚。

第5章 你的宠物,你的信徒

这时她脑袋突然咔嗒一下,"对讲机!"凯和菲尔异口同声地喊道。

"他在店子里!"菲尔大喊一声。"我一定是在……4个多小时以前回来时把他锁在里面了。"凯和菲尔就像救生员要去营救现场一样从后门向小店飞奔。

菲尔退休后,就在他们家后面搭了一间木工店。他一向喜欢做点木工活,虽然起初他只是想给朋友和家人做一些东西,但现在他还有了一点小生意。店子和家之间的对讲机装置让凯很容易在菲尔工作时和他讲话。她可以叫他回来吃午饭或是告诉他电话留言。

对讲机装置对孙子们同样好玩。他们互相讲话,就好像是在民用波段的无线电上讲话一样。每每听到从对讲机里传来的"10号呼叫4号,好兄弟,"或是"通话完毕",凯就会笑出声。但怎么现在他们在对讲机里听到了杰西的声音?这说不通,但这不能阻止凯在听到杰西的求救声后飞快地向它跑去。

当凯和菲尔经过小店的窗户时,他们被眼前看到的一幕惊呆了:杰西站在菲尔的椅子上。他一只前爪放在桌子上,但另一只却在按对讲机上的呼叫键,不知疲倦地大声叫着,以便有人能听见它的呼救。他们以前就知道杰西很聪明:它能在听到指示后握手或是汪汪叫。但它是怎么弄清楚对讲系统的?他们为他们小狗的机灵感到惊奇。让凯更感到惊讶的是,杰西在孤身被困数小时之后所表现出来的毅力和信任。它对着空中叫了多长时间?为什么这么长时间

迷失的小狗

没有反应它还一直在叫?

凯和菲尔推开门后,杰西跳了下来,跑去迎接他们。它跳到凯的怀里,带着感激和宽慰舔着她的脸。

"乖狗狗,"凯反复说着,紧紧抱着杰西,吻着他额头的棕色斑点。"菲尔,你要知道,杰西知道我们会来营救它。"她眼睛里还充满着泪水,继续说。"它所能做的全部的事,就是保证我们能听到它的声音——它知道那样就足以让我们找到它。"

菲尔同意地点了点头。很快,他心情就轻松起来,补充了一句,"你营救得很好;自从大学以后,我就没有看见你像那样跑过。"凯开玩笑地捶了一下她丈夫的肩膀。

那天晚上睡觉之前,凯对上帝祈祷,感谢他让杰西平安回家。她挠了挠小狗的耳朵后面,然后开始为她的儿子祈祷——和她以前千万次所作的祈祷一样。她又重新确信,上帝确实在倾听。才几小时前还重重压在她心里的孤独感和遗弃感现在已经消失了。取而代之的是安宁。

杰西没有放弃她会来救它的信念,即使似乎没有人听到、也没有人来。凯的心里充满了新的信心和信念。她也不会放弃。她相信上帝会听见她的祈祷,关心她和艾伦。她不会停止祈祷和对上帝的信任。

这就足够了。

6

Your Pet,
a Companion

6

你的宠物，你的伴侣

一只小麻雀掉到地上我也会知道。而你
比麻雀要贵重得多。我将你铭刻在我掌上，对
你了如指掌，你有多少根头发我也知道。你要
感到安慰：你绝不是一个人。我常和你同在。

永远的，
你的上帝和朋友

——源自《马太福音》10：29-31；
《以赛亚书》49：16；《马太福音》28：20

I even know when a little sparrow falls to the ground. And you're much more valuable. I've engraved you on the palms of My hands. I personally know you and have counted the very hairs of your head. Take comfort: You're never alone. Surely I am always with you.

Forever yours,
Your God and Friend

—from Matthew 10:29–31;
Isaiah 49:16; Matthew 28:20

Everyone needs a companion. Even when it's not so easy to admit that we do—when we act as though we've got it all together or when we think we don't need anyone or anything—God knows what we need. Sometimes our companions are other human beings, but many times they're not.

Our most loyal companions just might be our pets. These companions may not be able to mow the yard or wash the dishes, but they are roommates that help make our houses into homes. And it's those unquantifiable gifts that make them essential to our everyday lives.

Pets unquestionably do more for us than many people are willing to admit. Although they can't speak to us in words, they most assuredly

speak to us loudly in the little things they do for
us from day to day.

When your pet faithfully gives you that early
morning wake-up call, he's saying that you are
needed. When she enthusiastically barks and jumps to
greet you each time you come home, she's shouting,
"I missed you. I'm glad you're back! " When he's
never too busy to snuggle on the couch when
you're alone at night, he's letting you know that
you're loved and valued.

Today, take a moment to appreciate
your pets—even though they haven't once
taken out the trash. The little things
they do to enrich our lives make
them more than just pets:
They're bona fide, loving
companions.

每个人都需要陪伴。虽然要承认这一事实并不是很容易——虽然我们看起来沉着冷静、积极乐观，或是我们认为不需要任何人或任何事——但上帝知道我们需要什么。有时，我们的伴侣是其他人，但很多时候却不是。

我们最忠实的伴侣可能就是我们的宠物。这些伴侣可能不会打扫院子或是洗碗，但它们和我们住在一起，却能帮我们把房子变成家。正是它们那些不可计数的天赋，让它们对我们的日常生活至关重要。

毫无疑问，宠物为我们所做的，比许多人愿意承认的要多得多。虽然它们不

能用言语和我们讲话，但它们却非常

自信地通过日常给我们做的小事和我们大声交流。

　　当你的宠物早上忠实地叫你起床时，它说的是：有

人需要你。当你每次回家，它热情地叫着、跳着迎接你时，

它在大声说，"我想你。我很高兴你回来了！"当你晚上独

自一人时，它总有空陪你一起偎依在沙发上，它那是

让你知道，你受人爱戴和珍视。

　　今天，花点时间赏识你的宠物吧——

虽然它们从未给你倒过垃圾。它们

所做的丰富我们生活的小事

让它们不仅仅是宠物。

它们是真诚、忠

实　的　伴

侣。

By associating with the cat,
one only risks becoming richer.

◆

COLETTE

一个人和猫交往所冒的唯一风险
就是会变得更加富有。

——科莱特

Comforts of Home

"Mom, I've already told you, I don't need a pet," Jane hollered over her shoulder as she carried another suitcase to the car.

"It will be a companion," retorted Jane's mother with resolve. "I just can't send you off totally alone."

"A companion, a pet, a cat, a kitten—it doesn't matter what you call it, I don't want it." Jane tried again to assert her independence as she walked back up the steps to the house where she had lived all her life.

"Listen, Jane, you're still my little girl, even if you are going off to college in the Big City." Her mother tried again, pleading. "Take the kitten as a favor to me."

Jane chafed at the thought of needing anyone's help—especially her mother's "security blanket", the kitten. Jane had always possessed an independent spirit, and she was excited by the prospect of making it on her own at New York University after spending her freshman year at a smaller school in her hometown. But Jane also knew that her parents had doted on their only child and would undoubtedly miss their daily contact even more than she would. They had attended every concert, program, and sporting event Jane had ever participated in, video camera in hand. Now Jane suspected that her mother would stop at nothing short of actually getting into one: of Jane's suitcases to make sure her only child would be safe. *That would never do,* Jane thought to herself with a smile. Taking the kitten seemed like a good compromise.

"OK, OK, I'll take her." Jane relented. She couldn't help feeling a little guilty about leaving her parents in that big, old house all alone, even if the city was just three hours away from their home in upstate New York.

What would they do without me to worry about or to wait up for on the weekends, Jane thought as her mother placed the little kitten into her hands.

The creature was so tiny and delicate. Jane laughed to herself at the idea that this little kitten could do anything for her—what could a cat protect her from?

"What will you name her?" Jane's mom asked, smiling through the tears.

Jane looked away, struggling to keep from being engulfed by her mother's emotion. "Give me a break, Mom," she protested, gazing down at the little orange-and-white-striped kitten in her arms. "I just resigned myself to keeping the little fur ball—I'll think of a name for her once I get settled in."

Jane finished cramming her belongings into the last inches of space in her car just as her dad arrived home from work. He got out of his car with a questioning look on his face. That's when Jane realized her parents had collaborated about the kitten. "The answer is yes," Jane said, putting on an exaggerated air of self-sacrifice. "I'm taking the kitten."

Her dad smiled, looked relieved, and embraced Jane. "Are you ready to go?" he asked, still holding her tight.

"I was born ready," Jane kidded gently, sensing the deep emotion of her big-hearted dad.

Jane's dad held her at arm's length, then addressed Jane's mother: "Molly, our little girl is all grown up. She's going to do just fine on her own."

The three embraced one more time and kissed each other good-bye. Everyone cried, but Jane's tears of sadness mingled with tears of excitement. She climbed into her car with the kitten, backed out of the driveway, and watched her parents in the rearview mirror, waving until she had turned the corner.

Her first night in the empty little apartment she'd picked out with her parents during the summer was both thrilling and strangely lonely. She could hardly wait to begin her new independent life. While she felt a little nervous about living off campus and not knowing anyone, she knew she would make friends as soon as classes began. After sorting through the suitcases and boxes until almost midnight, she placed a towel in a box in the kitchen for the kitten's bed, then made a bed for herself by layering blankets on the carpet in the bedroom.

But Jane couldn't sleep. The incessant, plaintive meowing from the kitchen was heartrending. *My "companion" is the one that's lonely, not me,* Jane thought smugly, and she reluctantly brought the kitten to the bedroom. As they snuggled together on the blankets, Jane had to admit that the warmth she felt from the little animal was soothing. They both fell asleep quickly and slept peacefully together until the sun crept through the window.

Her first order of business was to buy some furniture with the money her parents had given her. Jane took her time getting ready but still was fully dressed and out the door before the furniture stores were open. She decided to find a restaurant nearby for some breakfast.

Chapter 6: Your Pet, a Companion

As she walked into a small coffee shop at the corner of her block, the young man behind the counter smiled warmly and took her order. By the time Jane had finished her breakfast, she had learned that he was a student at NYU and lived off campus nearby. He had also complimented her on her eyes, causing her to blush and fumble gracelessly fora suitable reply. She finally settled on "thank you," then excused herself, saying she had a lot to do.

Continuing on to a furniture store three blocks down, it didn't take her long to choose a red, slipcovered couch and a wooden and wrought-iron bed with a matching dresser and nightstand. They were totally different from the white wicker in her bedroom at home but seemed to fit her new life just right. She made arrangements to have the furniture delivered that afternoon, then headed back to her apartment. She'd check on the kitten and wait for her purchases to arrive.

Just before she had given up on getting the furniture that day, the deliverymen knocked on her door. They moved her furniture up the five flights of stairs and into her apartment with surprising ease.

Jane plopped down on her new sofa, excited to call her mom with the news of her day. But thoughts of the kitten stopped her—Mom would ask first about how the kitten was getting along and about what she had named her. Jane suddenly realized she hadn't seen or heard from the kitten since the deliverymen had left.

"Kitty," she called. Silence. Jane quickly searched the small apartment. *She must have escaped when the door was open,* Jane surmised. "I knew this cat was a bad idea," she mumbled as she headed out the door to search the halls and knock on doors.

The kitten was not in the hallway. No one answered when she knocked on the first couple of doors. An old woman answered the third but hadn't seen the cat, and a man's voice hollered at her to go away when she knocked on the fourth. Jane braced herself to knock at the final apartment on the hall. When its door slowly opened, she was shocked at what she saw.

"Well, what a surprise," said the familiar voice, with the same warm smile from the coffee shop that morning. Again, she stumbled over her words as she explained that her kitten was missing.

Her neighbor held up a finger, guiding Jane's eyes to the small kitchen where her kitten stood drinking from a bowl of water on the floor. "She was sitting at my doorstep when I came home from work this afternoon," he explained kindly. "I figured she had escaped from somewhere and someone would come looking for her." He headed toward the kitchen and motioned for Jane to step inside. "I've been calling her Molly. I guess that's not really her name, but it seemed to fit."

"Molly? That's my mom's name! " Jane replied, eyes wide in disbelief. "It's perfect! "

"My name is Scott," he said as he scooped up the kitten and handed her to Jane. "You escaped this morning without telling me yours."

"Oh—mine's Jane." She blushed, then added, "Thanks for taking care of Molly. I'm sorry for any inconvenience."

"No inconvenience at all. I love cats and have been thinking of getting one myself," Scott said with that smile that was beginning to make Jane feel weak at the knees. "Everyone needs a companion."

As Jane turned to leave, Scott offered, "I'm free tomorrow if you'd like me to show you around town."

Jane accepted the invitation eagerly—not too eagerly, she hoped. She said good-bye to Scott and went home. Holding her kitten close, she whispered a sincere "thank you" into Molly's small, furry ear. She snuggled with her kitten on her new, red sofa and dialed her parents' number. *Maybe,* Jane thought with a smile, *a companion isn't such a bad idea after all.*

hugs

家的慰藉

拥抱·爱——宠物总动员

"妈妈,我已经告诉你了,我不需要什么宠物,"简一边把另一个手提箱扛到车里,一边大声地抱怨道。

"它会是你的一个伙伴,"简的妈妈坚定地反驳。"我不能让你这样孤孤单单地离开。"

"一个陪伴,一只宠物,一只猫,一只小猫——不管你怎么叫它,我都不想要。"简又一次坚决地表明她的独立,往回走上台阶,回到她住了一辈子的家。

"听着,简,即便你是要到大城市里上大学,你仍然是我的小女儿。"她妈妈又尝试了一次,请求道,"把猫咪带上,就算是帮我的忙。"

对需要别人的帮助这一想法,简感到非常恼火——尤其是她

家 的 慰藉

妈妈给她的"安全毯",小猫。简一直都很独立,想到在她自己家乡的小学校读完大一之后要到纽约大学一个人生活,她兴奋不已。可简也知道,她的父母对她这个独生女非常宠爱,他们毫无疑问会比她更怀念他们平日在一起的时光。简参加过的每一次音乐会、节目和体育项目,他们都不会错过,并且手里总是拿着摄像机。现在,简怀疑她妈妈甚至要钻到她的行李箱里,才会确认她唯一的女儿会安全无事。"那可不行,"简笑着想。这样,把猫咪带上,对妈妈而言似乎是一个不错的承诺。

"好吧,好吧,我带上她。"简的脾气变得温和了一些。要把父母独自留在这陈旧的大房子里,她不禁感到有一点愧疚,尽管她要去的城市离她们在纽约州北部的家只有3小时的行程。妈妈把小猫咪放到她手中时,她心里想,"他们不用再担心我,也不用等我周末回家,那他们会做些什么呢?"

这只小猫是那么的瘦小、脆弱。想到这只小猫会给她做什么,简不禁笑了起来——小猫能保护她什么?

"你准备给她起什么名字?"简的妈妈含着眼泪笑着问。

简把头扭过去看着别处,挣扎着不让自己被妈妈的情感所吞噬。"让我休息一下,妈妈,"她抗议道,眼睛盯着怀里橙白相间的小猫。"我刚顺从了你的意思,留下这只小毛球——我一安顿好,就给她起个名字。"

第6章 你的宠物,你的伴侣

等到简的爸爸下班回来时,她已经将车子里最后几寸地方也塞满了行李。她爸爸从车里出来时,一脸质疑。这时,简才意识到,原来父母早已在小猫的问题上串通好了。"答案是,我会的,"简说,脸上带着夸张的自我牺牲的神情。"我会带走小猫。"

她爸爸笑了,看起来很宽慰,抱了一下简。"你准备好了吗?"他问,仍然紧紧地握着她的手。

"我一出生就准备好了,"简开了个小小的玩笑,体会到她那一向慷慨大方的爸爸的深情。

简的爸爸和她隔了有一手臂远的距离,对简的妈妈说,"莫利,我们的小姑娘已经长大了。她一个人会没事的。"

3个人又一次拥抱在了一起,相互吻别。每个人都哭了,但简的泪水里既有忧伤也有兴奋。她带着小猫钻到车里,把车从车道里倒出,在后视镜里注视着父母,挥着手,一直到她转弯。

她第一晚呆在空空的小公寓里,感到既兴奋又有点生疏和孤单,这个公寓是暑假她和父母一起挑选的。她迫不及待地想要开始她的独立新生活。虽然住在校外,什么人也不认识,她感到有一点点紧张,但她知道,一开课她就会交很多朋友。等她整理完行李,几乎到了半夜。她在厨房的一个盒子上放了一条毛巾,当做是小猫的床,然后在卧室的地毯上铺了一些毯子,给自己收拾了一张床。

但简却不能入眠。不断从厨房传出的悲哀的喵喵声令人心碎。

160

家 的 慰 藉

需要"陪伴"的是那个感到孤独的猫,不是我,简自鸣得意地想。她勉为其难地把小猫带到卧室里。当她们一起偎依在毯子上时,简不得不承认,她从这小家伙身上感到的温暖确实能起到一定的安慰作用。她们很快就入睡了,一直平静地睡到太阳爬到窗户上。

她起床后的首要大事就是用父母给她的钱买一些家具。简不紧不慢地做着准备,等到穿戴整齐、出了门,家具店还是没开门。于是,她决定先到附近找一家餐馆吃早点。

当她经过街脚的小咖啡店时,柜台后面的年轻小伙子热情地和她打招呼,给她点了菜。简用完早点,得知他也是纽约大学的学生,就住在附近学校外面。他对她的眼睛大加赞赏,让她感到不好意思,脸都红了,支支吾吾试图找到合适的回答。最后,她说了句"谢谢,"然后向他道别,说她还有好多事要做。

紧接着,她到了3个街区远的一家家具店,没过多久就挑了一件红色带套沙发和一张带有梳妆柜和床头柜的木铁床。它们和她自家卧室里的柳条家具完全不一样,但似乎和她的新生活很般配。她安排好让他们下午送货,然后就回到了公寓。她准备看看小猫,然后等着家具的到来。

正当她以为当天收不到家具时,送货员敲门了。他们非常自如地把家具搬到她住的5楼的公寓里,自如得令人惊讶。

简扑通一下坐在新买的沙发上,兴奋地想告诉妈妈当天发生的事。但一想到小猫，她就停住了——妈妈首先肯定会问小猫过得怎样，还有她给她起了什么名字。简突然意识到，自从送货员走了之后，她就没有看到或是听到小猫了。

"咪咪，"她喊道。一片寂静。简快速搜索着她的小公寓。"她一定是在门开着时跑出去了，"简猜测。"我就知道，带上这只猫是个糟糕的主意，"她一边出门在走廊上寻找、一家家敲门询问，一边咕哝道。

小猫不在走廊上。她先敲了两家的门，也没有人答应。到了第3家时，一个老太太答应了，却说没有看见猫。等她敲到第4家时，一个男人大声吼着，让她滚开。简打起精神，一直敲到最后一家。当门缓缓打开时，她被眼前的一切惊呆了。

"噢，真是太意外了！"和那天早上一样熟悉的声音，一样熟悉的热情的微笑。又一次，她不知道说什么好，只是解释说，她的小猫丢了。

她的邻居举起了一只手指，将简的视线指引到小厨房里，在那里，她的小猫正从地板上的碗里喝水。"我今天下午下班回来，她就坐在我家门口，"他亲切地解释。"我想，她一定是从什么地方逃出来的，一定会有人来找。"他朝厨房走去，示意简也进去。"我一直叫她莫利。我想那不是她的真名，但看起来似乎很合适。"

"莫利？那是我妈妈的名字！"简回答，眼睛瞪得大大的，几乎不敢相信。

"这真是太好了！"

"我叫斯科特，"他把猫抱起来递给了简。"你今天上午逃走了，连名字也没告诉我。"

"哦——我叫简。"她的脸红了，补充道，"谢谢你照看莫利。给你添麻烦了，真是过意不去。"

"一点也不麻烦。我喜欢猫，一直想给我自己找一只，"斯科特又微笑地说，那微笑让简感觉腿都软了。"每个人都需要一个陪伴。"

当简准备离开时，斯科特邀请道，"我明天有空，如果你愿意，我可以带你到处逛逛。"

简急切地接受了邀请——她希望不要显得太急切了。她和斯科特道别，回家了。她紧紧抱着她的小猫，轻轻地对着莫利小巧、毛茸茸的耳朵真诚地说了句"谢谢"。她和她的小猫一起偎依在她新买的红沙发上，拨通了父母的电话。"也许，"简笑着想，"有一个陪伴，并不是那么糟的想法。"

chapter

7

Your Pet,
a Giver

7

你的宠物，你的给予

人为朋友舍命，人的爱心没有比这个更伟大的。那就是我对你的爱。我是你的好牧人，愿意为你舍命。为他人舍命，是少有的。但真正不可思议的，是在你爱我甚至是认识我之前，我就已经为你舍弃了我自己。现在，我已向你展示了舍生之爱的很好的典范。即便如此，你也应该跟随我的榜样，为他人舍命。

不惜一切代价爱你的，

耶稣

——源自《约翰福音》15:13;《罗马书》5:7-8;
《约翰福音》10:11;《约翰一书》3:16

No greater love has ever been shown than when someone willingly gives his life for a friend. That's the kind of love I have for you. I am your Good Shepherd, willing to lay down My life to save you. It's rare for someone to give his life for another. But what's truly incredible is that I gave Myself for you before you loved Me or even knew Me. Now you have My perfect example of sacrificial love. Even so, you should follow My example and give your life for others.

Loving you at all costs,
Jesus

—from John 15:13; Romans 5:7–8;
John 10:11; 1 John 3:16

Have you ever witnessed a pure act of compassion, a true example of sacrificial love? If you've ever been at the right time and place to view such a gift, you know it will be forever etched in your memory and in your heart.

We've all heard stories of the dog that ran back into the burning building to save a child or who placed himself between a baby and a poisonous snake, willing to take the bite to save the little one. Dogs are famous for their faithfulness to the ones they love.

Pets sometimes remind us of the purity in loving actions. They don't weigh the odds or think about what would be best for them; they simply react, and in that reaction we are privileged to glimpse tree loyalty.

Jesus said, "Greater love has no one than this, that he lay down his life for his friends" (John 15:13). And even though He was talking about human love, that truth is often exemplified in our pets. They love us totally and completely, without reservation. Sometimes they give comfort, sometimes joy, or laughter, or even tears. But always they give us the gift of love, even at the cost of their own well-being.

God loves us that much too. His act of sending His Son to die for us is the ultimate example of sacrificial love, and once we've caught a glimpse of that powerful love, we can never be the same.

你曾目睹过纯粹的怜悯行

为和牺牲之爱的真实例子吗?如果你曾在适当的

时间和地点目睹这一馈赠,你就会知道,这会永远刻在

你的记忆深处和心里。

我们都听过这样的故事:一只狗跑到熊熊燃烧的大

楼里救了一个小孩,或是将自己挡在婴儿和毒蛇之间,

为了救小孩,宁愿自己被咬。狗正是以对他们所爱

戴的人的忠诚而闻名。

宠物有时让我们想起了爱心行动的

纯洁。他们不会权衡得失,或是思

考什么对他们最为有利;他

们只是作出反应,

从他们的

反应中，我们有幸目睹真正的忠实。

耶稣曾说，"人为朋友舍命，人的爱心没有比这个大的"（《约翰福音》15：13）。虽然他说的是人类的爱，但这一真理却在我们宠物身上得以体现。他们全心全意地爱我们，毫无保留。有时他们给予我们安慰，有时给予我们喜悦，或是笑声，或是眼泪。但它们总给予我们爱的馈赠，即使是以它们的健康为代价。

上帝也那样爱我们。他让他的圣子为我们而死，就是牺牲之爱最明显的例子，我们一旦瞥见那强有力的爱，就永远不会再和以前一样。

狗是这个世界上唯一爱你胜过爱他自己的生物。

——乔希·比林斯

A dog is the only thing on this earth
that loves you more than he loves himself.
◆

JOSH BILLINGS

Greater Love

A sick sense of dread gripped Ellen's heart. She could feel the unmistakable stickiness of blood on Sadie's foreleg and knew the guide dog was injured and in pain. Still, Sadie valiantly struggled to lead her master home safely, although slowed by a noticeable limp. Would Sadie's strength hold out long enough?

"Tom! " Ellen cried frantically when she and Sadie finally made it the two blocks to their own driveway after the terrible accident, Ellen heard the front door bang and the sweet sound of bare feet approaching through soft grass. She sensed her husband's presence and smelled his cologne even before she felt his gentle hands on her arms or heard his concerned voice.

"Ellen, you're hurt…," Tom said, inspecting her bloody hands.

"No, but Sadie is." Ellen collapsed into Tom's strong arms.

"What happened?" They both knelt by the panting dog now sprawled, exhausted and bleeding, on the grass of home and safety.

"I couldn't hear them until it was too late…boys on bicycles," Ellen gasped. "They must have come around the corner just as we started to cross the street…going way too fast… Tom, there was nothing we could do! "

"They didn't even stop to help you?" Ellen could hear disbelief and anger in Tom's voice.

"Sadie knocked me down," Ellen continued breathlessly. "Back onto the sidewalk. She saved me, Tom…but she couldn't save herself." Ellen sniffed loudly.

"They were so close I could feel the wind from their bikes as they passed by," she continued, her chin quivering with emotion. "It was terrifying! Then I heard a sickening thump, and Sadie yelped in pain ··· I knew she had sacrificed herself for me..." Ellen sobbed, finally allowing the fear and feelings of helplessness to spill over her thin veneer of control. "Oh, Tom, how bad is she? Is she...is she going to be OK?"

"I don't know," Tom admitted, turning his attention to the heroic dog. "Let's get her to the vet's office fast."

Ellen crawled into the backseat of the car. She could hear Tom strain with exertion as he lifted the big dog gently onto the seat beside her. She cradled Sadie's head tenderly in her lap as Tom left to get his shoes and lock up the house.

"You're a good girl," Ellen whispered soothingly. "You've been the best guide dog and friend I could ever have wanted." Hot tears stung Ellen's cheeks, and she buried her face in Sadie's fur. "Thank you. Thank you for everything you've ever done for me—for everything you've given."

Ellen desperately hoped this wouldn't be good-bye.

She remembered how small and frightening her

world had been before Sadie had "rescued" her more than eight years ago. Since then, Sadie had been more than Ellen's eyes; she had been her heart.

Ellen loved having Sadie with her. The dog had seen Ellen through countless trials and difficulties. She had guided her through town; through grocery stores and malls; through Disney World and many other family vacations; and through her days as a teacher, wife, and mom.

She was proud of the magnificent way Sadie operated. People were inspired when they saw the beautiful; intelligent dog at work. Sadie was always on call, always ready to get up and go whenever Ellen needed her, eager to guide and protect.

Even at rest, Sadie had always been perfect—sitting patiently, not distracted by other things or people, and always gentle and patient with excitable children. German shepherds were known for their strong character, their uncanny intelligence, and their faithfulness. Sadie had exemplified all the best traits of her breed every day of her life.

Now, as Sadie groaned softly and gently licked her own blood from Ellen's hands, Ellen couldn't help but note the irony: Sadie's blood was on her hands. She felt miserably guilty and responsible for what had happened. Why had she taken her walking on the busy city streets so soon? Sadie had only resumed her guiding role a few days ago—after recovering from her recent eye surgery. But Ellen had been so glad to have her back and just wanted to get back to normal. They had always enjoyed their evening walks together. Now she had to face the possibility that things might never be normal again.

Tom was back. She heard his seat belt click shut and the whine of the mirror moving. She guessed he was making sure he could check on her and Sadie as he drove. His care and concern warmed Ellen's heart. But even those thoughts reinforced her feelings of guilt.

It had been Tom who had first broached the subject that maybe it was time for Ellen to think about getting a new guide dog. Ellen had flatly refused to listen to his gentle suggestions that the ten-year-old dog's growing health problems were slowing her down and making her work difficult. Ellen didn't want to think of Sadie's growing old. She didn't ever want to give up the smooth and wonderful working relationship—not to mention the close personal bond with this wonderful dog. So what if Sadie wasn't as fast as she used to be? She was still far faster than Ellen was, and that was enough. A little arthritis? Even Ellen had a little arthritis, but she kept going, and so would Sadie.

Sure, there had been the eye problems. But dogs of any age could get eye infections, right? And after the surgery, Sadie could see fine.

Tom was silent as they drove, but she could feel his eyes on her—boring into her. He didn't say it now, and she appreciated that, but he didn't have to. She knew what he was thinking.

Had she missed the signs that it was time for Sadie to retire? Had she waited too long? Would Sadie have to pay the ultimate price because Ellen had selfishly refused to see the handwriting on the wall and let her faithful friend and guide go?

She gently kissed Sadie's head as Tom stopped the car, got out, and opened the back door. "Hang in there, girl," she encouraged. Ellen winced when Sadie yipped as Tom picked her up. "Careful!" Ellen admonished. "It's OK, Sadie, the doctor is here. You'll be OK," she promised.

◆

"She'll be OK, Ellen," the doctor announced after more than one insufferable hour in the waiting room. "I promise."

Ellen clapped her hands and laughed with relief. Tom put his hands on her shoulders and squeezed supportively.

"She'll need surgery to repair damage to her shoulder and set that broken leg … she'll have to stay here for a few days, but she should heal just fine."

"Thank you, Doctor." Ellen reached out to touch the doctor's arm appreciatively. She heard him pull up a chair to face hers and knew he had something serious to say. She was convinced Tom and the doctor were communicating silently with their eyes and facial expressions. It was unnerving to be left out of the loop when Sadie was *her* dog.

"We have to talk about Sadie's future," the doctor said in a calm, nonconfrontational tone. "She won't heal as fast as she did when she was young," he warned. "She'll have to stay off her feet for a few weeks." Ellen nodded. "And you'll have to get along without her for even longer than that—like after the eye surgery."

He paused, and Ellen remembered the difficult adjustment that had been. It had meant a return to the difficult days with a cane before Sadie had come along. The cane didn't come when she called it and was easily misplaced. Stairs were frightening, and people seemed to shy away from her with the cane rather than being drawn to Sadie's friendly personality. Ellen had hated that time, but she knew she could get through it if she had to. And now she had to.

Suddenly she knew what she needed to do. Sadie had sacrificed herself for Ellen time and time again, and now it was time for Ellen to return the favor. An act of pure, sacrificial love had brought about Sadie's injury. Now Ellen's love for her dog made this decision unavoidable...but no less difficult.

The doctor cleared his throat to speak again, but Ellen spoke first. "It's OK. Sadie can take all the time she needs to recuperate and rest," she announced. "It's time for Sadie to retire. She has served my interests well for eight years. Now it's time I served hers."

Tom put his arms around her. He and the doctor both talked at once. "She'll always be a treasured part of the family—," Tom said.

"You can apply for another guide dog immediately," the doctor was saying. "It won't be the same, but—"

"No one could ever replace Sadie," Tom agreed.

Surprisingly, Ellen felt good about her decision. She knew it was the right one for Sadie, the dog who exemplified faithfulness, loyalty, and sacrificial love. Ellen suddenly began to relish the thought of her beloved dog being able to relax, lazing around the house doing normal dog things. She laughed at the thought of Sadie ever being normal. She was—and always would be—a most extraordinary dog.

为爱奋不顾身

　　埃伦心里有一种恶心的恐惧。她清楚地感觉到萨迪前腿流血了，黏糊糊的，知道她的向导犬受伤了，很痛苦。但萨迪仍然勇敢地挣扎着将她的主人安全地带回家，虽然走起路来明显一瘸一拐，速度很慢。萨迪有力气坚持足够长时间吗？

　　埃伦和萨迪在那次可怕的车祸后，走了两个街区，最终到了自家的车道，埃伦疯狂地喊，"汤姆！"埃伦听到前门砰的响了一声，接着是赤脚在软草上走过的甜美的声音。在她感觉到丈夫把他温柔的手搭在她胳膊上，或是听到他关切的声音之前，她就感觉到了丈夫的存在，闻到了他古龙香水的味道。

　　"埃伦，你受伤了……"汤姆说，审视着她血淋淋的手。

第7章 你的宠物,你的给予

"不,是萨迪受伤了。"埃伦倒在了汤姆坚实的臂膀里。

"发生什么事了?"他们俩一同跪在气喘吁吁的向导犬旁,她现在四肢伸展着,躺在家里安全的草地上,筋疲力尽,还流着血。

"等我听到他们时已经太晚了……那些骑在自行车上的男孩子们,"埃伦喘息着说。"正当我们准备过马路时,他们一定是在拐弯……骑得太快了……汤姆,我们什么办法也没有!"

"他们甚至都没有停下来帮你?"埃伦从汤姆的声音里听到了怀疑和愤怒。

"是萨迪把我扑倒的,"埃伦继续说,还没喘过气来。"把我扑倒了人行道上。她救了我,汤姆……可她却不能救她自己。"埃伦大声抽泣着。

"他们离得太近了,他们经过时,我都可以听得见他们自行车上的风声,"她继续说,脸颊激动地颤抖着。"太恐怖了!然后,我就听见令我眩晕的扑通声,接着萨迪就痛苦地尖叫起来……我知道,她为我牺牲了自己……"埃伦哽咽起来,害怕和无助的情感最终溢了出来,再也控制不住了。"噢,汤姆,她伤得怎样?她会……没事吧?"

"我不知道,"汤姆回答,把注意力转向英勇的狗那里。"我们快点把她送到兽医那儿。"

为爱奋不顾身

埃伦爬到车里的后座上。她能听到,汤姆把狗轻轻地抱到她座位旁时非常费劲。当汤姆回屋取鞋子关门时,她把萨迪的头温柔地搁在她的膝盖上。

"你是个好孩子,"埃伦安慰地小声说。"你是我能拥有的最好的向导犬和朋友。"热泪刺痛了埃伦的脸颊,她把脸埋在萨迪的软毛里。"谢谢你。谢谢你为我做的一切——你给我的一切。"

埃伦绝望地希望,这不会是永别。

她记起,在萨迪8年前"挽救"她之前,她的世界是如此的渺小和可怕。从那以后,萨迪就不仅仅是埃伦的眼睛了;她是她的心。

埃伦喜欢有萨迪在身边。这条狗帮她渡过了无数的难关。她带她穿过市镇;带她到杂货店和购物广场;带她到迪斯尼乐园,以及度过许多其他的家庭假期;帮她度过作为老师、妻子和母亲的日子。

她为萨迪在执行使命时所表现出的优美举止感到骄傲。人们看到这只漂亮、聪明的狗在工作时,很受启发。萨迪总是随叫随到,极力渴望提供指引和保护。

即使在休息时,萨迪也是无可挑剔——耐心地坐着,不受任何人或事的干扰,对容易兴奋的小孩也总是温柔、耐心。德国牧羊犬以它们坚强的性格、出奇的智慧和忠实而闻名。而这一品种里所有好的特性，都在萨迪生活的每一天得以完美的体现。

现在，萨迪轻声地呻吟着，温柔地从埃伦手上将自己的血舔下来，埃伦不禁感到一种讽刺。萨迪的血竟然在她手上。她对所发生的事情感到内疚，觉得应该为此事负责。她为什么要这么快就带着它在繁忙的城市街道上行走？萨迪几天前才刚刚恢复它的指引角色——刚从最近的眼部手术恢复。但能让它回来工作，埃伦是那么的高兴，只想让一切都恢复正常。她们总是喜欢晚上一起散步。现在，她必须要面对这样一个可能，那就是，事情也许再也不会恢复正常了。

汤姆回来了。她听到他的安全带咔的一声关上了，还有镜子唧唧转动的声音。她猜想，他是想确保他能在行驶过程中盯着她和萨迪。他的照顾和关心温暖了埃伦的心。但即使是思考这些，还是加深了她的愧疚感。

汤姆首先提到过这个话题，他觉得埃伦也许该考虑重新认领一条新的向导犬。他说，现在已经１０岁的萨迪有越来越多的健康问题，这让它行动变慢了，工作也费劲了，可埃伦断然拒绝听从他友善的建议。埃伦不想考虑萨迪在变老这一事实。她不想放弃她们之间和谐美妙的工作关系——更别提与这只出色的狗之间亲密的个人感情了。萨迪没有以前那么快，那又怎样？它仍然比埃伦要快，那就足够了。它有一点关节炎？可埃伦也有一点关节炎，但她还是继续在走路，萨迪也会的。

当然，还有眼睛的问题。但任何年龄的狗都有可能眼部感染，对吗？动了手术后，萨迪看东西就没有问题了。

一路上，汤姆都沉默不语，但埃伦能感觉到他在注视她——像要把她穿透一样。他现在什么也没有说，埃伦对此很感激，但他也不必这样做。她知道他在想什么。

她没有看到萨迪该退休的迹象吗？她等待的时间太长了吗？就是因为埃伦自私地拒绝看清这不祥之兆，不让她忠实的朋友和向导离开，萨迪就要付出这么惨重的代价吗？

汤姆停车时，她轻轻地吻了吻萨迪的头，开了后门、下了车。"挺住，女孩，"她鼓励道。汤姆把萨迪抱起时，萨迪尖叫了一声，埃伦惊了一下。"小心点！"埃伦提醒道。"没事的，萨迪，医生在这儿。你会没事的，"她向它保证。

◆

"她会没事的，埃伦，"在等候室待了难熬的一个多小时之后，医生宣布。"我向你保证。"

埃伦鼓起掌来，宽慰地笑了。汤姆把手搭在她的肩膀上，支持地拥抱了她一下。

第7章 你的宠物,你的给予

"它需要做手术来修复肩部的损伤,还有那只断了的腿……它要在这儿呆上几天,但她应该会恢复得不错的。"

"谢谢你,医生。"埃伦伸出手,感激地握住了医生的胳膊。她听见他拖了一把椅子对着她坐下,知道他有很重要的话要说。她深信,汤姆和医生正在默默地用眼神和面部表情交流着。萨迪是她的狗,但她却对它的情况一无所知,这让她很紧张。

"我们必须谈谈萨迪的将来,"医生用冷静、非对抗的语气说。"它不会和它年轻时恢复得一样快,"他警告说。"它要卧床好几周。"埃伦点了点头。"你得要有更长一段时间学着适应没有它的日子——就像它动了眼部手术一样。"

他停了停,这时,埃伦记起了那艰难的适应期。这意味着又要回到以前萨迪没有到来、要用拐杖的艰难的日子。当她叫唤的时候,拐杖不能自己过来,并且还容易放错地方。楼梯也很吓人,并且当她拄着拐杖时,人们似乎总是回避她,而不是像萨迪在身边时被她那友好的性格吸引。埃伦讨厌那样的日子,但她知道,如果实在必须的话,她也能挺过去。现在她也必须这样做。

突然,她知道她需要做什么了。萨迪一次次地为埃伦牺牲她自己,现在轮到埃伦回报这一恩惠了。正是因为纯粹的牺牲自我的行为,才导致萨迪受伤。现在,埃伦对她的爱犬的爱使得这一决定不可避免……但仍然很艰难。

医生清了清嗓子,准备继续讲话,但这次是埃伦先开口。"没关系。萨迪尽管恢复和休息,需要多长时间都可以,"她宣布。"萨迪是该退休了。她已经很好地为我服务了 8 年。现在该我为她服务了。"

汤姆搂住了她。他和医生同时劝说她。"它将永远是家里珍贵的一员——,"汤姆说。

"你可以马上再申请另一只向导犬,"医生说。"不会一模一样,但——"

"没有人可以取代萨迪,"汤姆表示赞同。

令人吃惊的是,埃伦对她所作的决定感觉很好。她知道,她为萨迪——这只体现了忠实、忠心和牺牲之爱的狗——作出了正确的决定。埃伦突然开始回味这一想法:她的爱犬可以轻松了,懒散地在家里做一些普通狗做的事情。想到萨迪竟然会变得普通,她不禁笑了。她是——也永远会是—— 一只最不寻常的狗。